It wasn't hard to figure out who done it. You'll not the least surprised. A for sure modern day gothic. A very gothic novel. Pretty good as none to her stosia okce,

From Out of the Shadows

The altar was a huge block of stone with
the solid, eternal look of Stonehenge.
Above it a gigantic crucifix of some
greenish metal was precariously balanced on
a wooden block. With its enormous dark
space, its endless corners as secret as the
grave, this heart of the abbey filled me with
a peculiar horror that was half fascination.
Somewhere water dropped upon stone in
even, little splashes, sounding like faint,
distant footsteps, and suddenly—
There was a rush of icy air, and I screamed
as something huge and black came crashing
down on me. . . .

Other SIGNET Gothics You'll Want to Read

If you wish to order these titles,
please see the coupon in
the back of this book.

Night at Sea Abbey

by

Virginia Coffman

Ⓢ

A SIGNET BOOK

NEW AMERICAN LIBRARY

TIMES MIRROR

NAL BOOKS ARE ALSO AVAILABLE AT DISCOUNTS IN BULK
QUANTITY FOR INDUSTRIAL OR SALES-PROMOTIONAL USE.
FOR DETAILS, WRITE TO PREMIUM MARKETING DIVISION,
NEW AMERICAN LIBRARY, INC., 1301 AVENUE OF THE
AMERICAS, NEW YORK, NEW YORK 10019.

 SIGNET TRADEMARK REG. U.S. PAT. OFF. AND FOREIGN COUNTRIES
REGISTERED TRADEMARK—MARCA REGISTRADA
HECHO EN CHICAGO, U.S.A.

SIGNET, SIGNET CLASSICS, MENTOR, PLUME AND MERIDIAN BOOKS
are published by The New American Library, Inc.,
1301 Avenue of the Americas, New York, New York 10019

First Signet Printing, June, 1978

1 2 3 4 5 6 7 8 9

PRINTED IN THE UNITED STATES OF AMERICA

For those special fans and friends:
Myra K, Robin D.S., Karri C., Robin G.,
and Samuel R.B.—with many thanks.

ONE

Hoping for a break in the weather, I had waited until noon before heading out of London for the West Country, but the depressing gray mist preceded me through the midlands and Somerset, only raising its curtain for a dazzling sunset when I reached Bristol Channel. Although the gaudy orange light nearly blinded me as I drove toward the village of Abbeyvue, paralleling the channel, my spirits thawed in the bright, windy afternoon, and I lost most of my uneasiness over the wedding to which I had been invited as the sister of the bridegroom, and his only relative.

When Bob invited me to his wedding at some ancient place called Sea Abbey on a tiny island in Bristol Channel, he was embarrassingly insistent about one thing: "Emily's family may be broke when it comes to money and junk like that, but the Calders have got this abbey that's been in the family since the tenth century, and their family is so old they make us Yankee Garrisons sound like monkeys just out of the trees . . . So you see," he added naively, "they can't possibly be after my—pardon, Sis—your money."

"Of course not," I had agreed with suitable enthusiasm, because I could tell from his voice how deliriously happy he was in his engagement to seventeen-year-old Emily Calder, the English girl he had met that summer at a Mediterranean Club camp-out.

But that phone call to me at the Hotel Meurice in Paris had been made two weeks ago, to explain why he was going to remain as a houseguest—abbeyguest?—of the Calders on their microscopic Isle of Mundy in Bristol Channel, which they called Sea Abbey.

Later, when I reached London after some Paris shopping, there were calls from both Bob and excited, bubbly young Emily, a child I liked at once, from the contagious youth and gaiety in her voice. These calls focused on the wedding arrangements, details of their future married life, and the invitation to me to be a guest at Sea Abbey for the small wedding which would be private, owing to the death early that summer of the family's matriarch, called "Granny" Calder by young Emily.

"She fell out of a window, or whatever they have in abbeys," Bob had confided to me in a stage whisper on the phone. "That's why they sent Emily to the Mediterranean Club. To forget. And then—" he added rapturously, "—we met!"

"Exactly like on the telly," Emily put in, apparently over Bob's shoulder. "But darling Granny would have adored Bob. And anyway, we just have to get married as soon as possible."

"What!" I cried, a good deal startled.

They had both laughed and Bob explained, "Not for *that* reason, Nell! But because we can't be apart, now that we've met at last."

I was amused that their "at last" should appear when she was seventeen and Bob nineteen, but I was determined not to be a spoilsport just because I had lost my own fiance years ago in a Navy helicopter crash. Now, at the age of thirty-one I was considered by the society pages and *Women's Wear Daily* as

"Nell Garrison, perennial bachelor girl who refuses to share Mama's millions with a Mr. Nell Garrison." Which was not the case at all. I simply hadn't met the man who would *not* be Mr. Nell Garrison.

I had spent some of those years acting as guardian to my young brother, Bob, but now I was not about to play the heavy stage mother with Bob and Emily. To tell the truth, much as I adored my delightful young brother, I felt a tiny sense of freedom at the thought that I need no longer constantly consider his plans before my own. It was selfish, but it was true. So I had cheered on the youngsters, discussed the wedding via phone with Emily's smooth-talking father, and agreed that Bob and Emily should have a large trust fund "cushion" just to tide them over until Bob's twenty-first birthday and the coming into his own considerable estate. But I had made one proviso, that Bob finish his final college year at the Sorbonne. He would now, of course, be accompanied to Paris by his bride.

I was fast approaching a steep, cliffside village whose tiny, semi-circular harbor below proved to be opposite a forbidding gray edifice looming out of the now fiery sunset waters of Bristol Channel. So huge was the abbey, about a mile offshore, and so small the island itself that for a moment my big sunglasses played me false and I thought the abbey rose directly out of the channel waters themselves, like some gray-shelled monster pushing up from the depths of the sea.

This was the ancestral home of the Calder family, whose walls were so ancient they made us Garrisons appear like Neanderthal man by comparison. It was impressive enough, but even at this distance across the choppy waters I suspected that as a family home it was neither endearing nor comfortable.

Half-blinded by the sunset, I managed to locate the garage at the edge of Abbeyvue, having been warned that it was impossible to drive further, as the village consisted of one cobbled street tilted straight downward to the miniature harbor and its stone quay. I found that Abbeyvue had much of the charm of the better known Clovelly in nearby Devonshire. Nevertheless, as the uncommunicative garageman pulled my two cases out of the trunk of the car and set them on the cobblestones, I was keenly aware of my status as an outlander, a foreigner in this tightly knit, proud little village.

Heavily dressed passersby, male and female, gave me brief, curious glances as they went up and down the steep street. In their dark jackets, their stiff boots, and strong, forbidding faces, they reminded me of Yorkshire friends I had known, long-wearing friends, but neither easy to know nor quick to accept the breezy, smiling, temporary people from the great cities.

I thanked the garageman and took up my cases. He disapproved, but did not stop me.

"Your man should be carrying them . . . Your husband, I mean to say."

"How true!" I agreed, which finally made him smile. One of his front teeth was missing but in no way detracted from his likable appearance. I said, "My brother is meeting me here at five o'clock. That should be at any moment. He will help me."

"Ay. That'll be more like it. You leave 'em here. Send your brother up for 'em."

"Thank you. I will." I set down the larger case and took the other which contained my makeup, jewelry and lingerie. But as I started down the cobbled little street, seeing that monstrous abbey shadowing the waters of the channel beyond the bay, I shivered under the sharp, autumnal wind.

A few dark-clad fishermen in shiny mackinaws and modern raincoats were busy about the quay. A boat no bigger than a dory and with an old, sputtering motor nosed in toward the. quay. A big brawny man leaped ashore, and tied up the boat to a metal loop. I recognized Bob as he too stepped ashore, dark and lithe and young, healthily enjoying all this marine activity. The big man was a veritable giant, his bright coppery hair looking as if it had never been combed. His beat-up khaki clothes looked as though they had been slept in. And I could see as I approached that his amiable, friendly face, fringed with a short, red beard, also looked unkempt and ruddy with outdoor life.

There was an older brother in the Calder family. Two brothers, if one could believe laughing young Emily, who had added slyly, "Of course, Keith's supposed to be our cousin, but once when Mother was frightfully done in at Papa, she told me Keith was what she called a 'nasty byblow of Pa's.' "

Emily had stopped then, laughed into the phone, and added, "But never mind Keith. He does all the work, so he's very rough-tempered. He may not even like Bob at all. We don't know yet. It's that dear old giant, my brother Duncan, you will like. Everyone does."

So this amiable young bearded giant was Emily's legitimate brother, Duncan Calder! He looked like a useful sort to have around the seashore, however unlikely to be found in an abbey. I waved and Bob saw me and shouted, and started running toward me. A stiff run over those maddening cobbles and almost straight up. I waved him back, laughing because he looked so young, yelling something about Emily and why she couldn't come and had I enjoyed my ride down from London.

"Yes, yes. For heaven's sake, don't run! You'll get heart failure running up this awful street," I called as I reached the bottom of the hill, but my complaint about their street earned me some surly looks from the inhabitants.

Bob threw his arms around me, still happily talking about Emily. "She's such a darling, you know! She meant to come over with us but she got an upset stomach or something and just couldn't make it."

"Bridal nerves!" called the grinning giant as he joined us. "Bobbin, do the decent, Old Boy!"

We all laughed as Bob, flustered, said, "Oh, sure! Dunc—that is, Duncan, this is . . . No, it's the other way around. Elinor, this is Dunc. Duncan. We call him Dunc."

"I gathered that," I agreed, with an amused glance at the bearded giant.

Bob said, "That's right. A great hulk, isn't he? He'd make a terrific linebacker for the Forty-Niners."

"That is a football team," I explained to Duncan, who gave me a delightfully toothy grin and admitted, "I suspected it, but I've no objection. I take it a linebacker is important to the game."

Bob was his enthusiastic self, superficially, but I thought there was an almost overdone excitement in his voice, as if he wanted to cover some fear, some unsureness. The realization troubled me but he went on loudly, clapping Duncan Calder on the back, "Absolutely essential!"

The bearded giant grinned and took my arm while Bob removed my Gucci case from my hand.

"Where's the rest of your wardrobe, Sis? I know you. You're no Club Camp-Out."

I explained that I had left it outside the garage and, as Duncan Calder took my smaller bag from him, Bob went galloping up the street while I yelled, "Don't run uphill like that! You want to get a heart attack?"

"At his age they never heard of heart attacks," Duncan told me, in his friendly way. "We're all very fond of your brother, Miss Garrison. And Emily has never been happier. She deserves happiness, poor little twit! Our grandmother's death took her rather badly. Best thing in the world for her now, meeting young Bobbin."

I asked, "How is your sister, Mr. Calder? I hope she is better."

"Nerves. Nothing but nerves. Came down sick after she'd been served her breakfast. Probably ate too fast. Come along to the boat. Not much of a vessel, but . . ." He shrugged as we crossed the quay. It was difficult to keep up with his long strides. "Some day, when the Calders are rich as Croesus, we hope to get a decent little vehicle. You know. Nothing like the Royal Yacht but something rather special. Bobbin thinks we might—"

If he had not broken off so suddenly, I would have noticed nothing. In the circumstances my suspicions were aroused at once. I tried not to make it obvious as I gave him a furtive side glance.

"In any case, we should have a decent little ship-shape vessel shortly after the wedding," he finished.

I said "I see!" in casual tones, but fortunately Bob came clattering down the hill at that minute and we stopped to wait for him. The subject did not come up again until we were under way. Duncan startled me by lifting me down into the dory as if I were a child. He was so gallant I could hardly fault him merely because he trailed my overnight case in the water and finished the job by swinging the case back up into the boat, splashing my Givenchy redingote with oily water.

"I can't wait for you to see her," Bob began while Duncan got the stubborn, ancient motor started.

"Who?" I asked, trying for a humor that eluded Bob who cried in a shocked voice,

"Emily, of course! My Emily!"

Duncan laughed and repeated to me in his jovial way, "Bobbin's Emily, of course."

He and I were still amused and Bob briefly incensed when Duncan got the motor going and we suddenly shot out into the rapidly shadowing waters of the little harbor. I fell against Duncan and we apologized, but I was secretly rather relieved that the first Calder I met should be so likable, so easy to know.

"Well, Bob, I'll be meeting her in no time at all. That is—" I added with a laughing glance at Duncan who had begun to fool with the off-sounding motor again—"if our transportation holds out."

Bob called, "Good Lord, Dunc! Don't tell me we're going to go floating around Bristol Channel for the night. Emily will have a fit. She's dying to see you, Nell."

I said, "I'm awfully sorry she was sick today. Is she feeling all right now?"

"Better, anyway. She was sick as a dog this morning. What the devil did happen to the poor kid, Dunc? I was half crazy until she came out of it along about noon."

Duncan had been intent upon the motor's clanking sound but he looked around and I was surprised and disconcerted at his slow, deep scowl.

"Granny's death shook her rather badly. But she doesn't get sick to her stomach like that."

I was puzzled to note that Duncan's scowl deepened, probably because he was worried about the motor.

I pulled up the military collar of my too-thin redingote as the wind roared over the channel, slapping our hair against our faces, twisting the ash blonde length of my own hair like Medusa's coils, which may have been all right when I was twenty, but at thirty-one I wore it in a loosely modern French twist. So between holding my vagrant hair and my coat collar, I missed the first little byplay of talk between the two men:

"Don't bother about it," Bob was saying. "Forget the idiot motor. The minute Emy and I are married I'll get my settlement, and you'll have your yacht, or cabin cruiser or whatever. You sure need it, out on that rock."

Duncan's laugh was short. "I'm afraid that won't go down well with Keith. You know how stubborn that brother—that cousin of mine can be."

Bob said easily, "We'll override his objections. It's just pride. Besides, I'll be one of the family then. He won't have anything to say about it."

"Who is—" I began, then remembered that Duncan Calder had an illegitimate brother who apparently lived and worked at the abbey. This, undoubtedly, was the stubborn Keith who was too proud to accept expensive favors from very new in-laws. I could not help respecting the stubborn Keith.

I glanced over at Duncan Calder and saw his bright, ruddy face was suddenly shadowed. Startled, I felt the chill of night pass across the boat and looked around quickly. Behind me loomed the great, stone monster that was Sea Abbey.

TWO

I was not the only one to look up at that ominous rock with something like dread. I saw Bob raise his head, his face in shadow, and he shivered, perhaps from the cold. As Duncan reduced speed we moved parallel to the long shoreline of the island, though I saw nothing but sheer rock climbing skyward until it seemed to form the towers and turrets of the abbey itself, a monumental object which appeared to be carved out of one miraculous chunk of stone.

The current knocked us hard against the rock and I disgraced myself by crying out, but Duncan assured me easily, "Old Keith will have seen us. Don't worry Miss—Nell. There! Behind you, at the top of the steps."

I looked around while holding so tightly to my board seat that my knuckles were white. A flight of stone steps rose out of the channel, the lowest steps scummed and covered by the oily green waters. On the narrow landing at the top a man stood watching our approach. He was of middle height, in his mid-thirties, I thought, lean and hard-faced, his faintly graying bronze hair blowing in the wind. Without even seeing them, I suspected that his eyes were fiercely, intolerantly blue. He was wearing short sleeves and khaki shorts, which took either courage or masochism in this wind. He had long, sturdy legs, if one admired the almost excessively masculine male.

"Any trouble?" this fellow called out to Duncan as he came down the unprotected and well-worn steps toward our approaching boat.

Bob threw him a line which he caught deftly as Duncan cut off the motor and we bumped with the tide against the lower steps. Duncan called, "We nearly konked out, as Young Bobbin says. We need a new boat."

"We need some work on the motor," Keith Calder corrected him. "There is nothing wrong with the boat." He gave me his hand to get me out of the rocking, swaying little dory, and I greeted him with what I hoped was a warm "Good afternoon," and "Thank you," but as he looked me over with those predictably blue eyes, I could see he hadn't much use for my fine Paris wardrobe, which was obviously out of place on a little dory whose bottom was paved with bilge water. He did have the decency to say, "Good evening, Miss Garrison," before he turned to hear his brother's more flattering comment about me. The bearded young giant, leaping to the step, remarked,

"We'll make a sailor out of Nell—Miss Garrison—yet. She took that step rather neatly; don't you think so, Keith? By the way, Nell, this is my—cousin, old Keith."

I started to extend my gloved hand, but of course, Keith Calder was busy lifting my bags out and either did not see my hand or ignored it.

"How is Emily?" Bob asked with anxious intensity.

"Doing well enough to entertain that death's-head scholar from Psychic Research," Keith said as he started up the steps with my bags while I followed, feeling unwanted and decidedly out of place. "Nothing to worry about for the moment," he added to

Bob. "She is giving our psychic friend a very bad time." One thing cheered me and that was the quick, surprisingly warm smile with which Keith relieved my brother's fears. I could forgive this proud, indifferent fellow a good deal for his obviously understanding and sympathetic treatment of the young lovers. All considered, one would not have suspected it of him.

Poor Bob rushed up the steps, passing us rather nervewrackingly on the outside where there was no bannister, no safety rail. Simply a terrible plunge straight down to the foaming waters far below. I had long since stopped saying "Don't do that!" to my young brother. He was old enough to look after his own safety. Nevertheless, his haphazard run up those slippery steps gave me a brief bad moment.

It was the genial Duncan who laughed at my expression as I looked down at the depths below and shuddered, but curiously enough, it was Keith Calder, the unfriendly, the indifferent, who took my wrist and more or less got between me and the rugged death that waited below. I thanked him at the top of the steps on the landing but he merely gazed at me thoughtfully with those forbidding, yet curiously fascinating sea-blue eyes.

At the island end of the landing was a big stone arch with a narrow door studded by metal including the great, rusted lock. All around that arch rose the gray walls with few openings, even for windows, so far as I could see. Far above, I made out little apertures, few and set within deep-cut stone several stories above us.

But the men were waiting for me. I hurried to join them. Bob had already rushed through the narrow door and disappeared beyond.

"Ah, love!" Duncan laughed at my brother's enthusiasm to meet his beloved Emily, and I joined sympathetically in that laugh. However, I noted as we passed through the little door that Keith did not find our amusement contagious. From the beginning of the conversation about Emily, I thought, Keith had been serious about her illness. I wondered for the first time if there was more to that sickness than mere "bridal nerves." It would be terribly disappointing to these young people, within days of their wedding, if young Emily should have some internal trouble, appendicitis, or an ulcer, or something else that would delay the ceremony.

Already the last rays of the sun were gone and the world of the channel lay in shadows. There was a blue dusk hanging over the little courtyard within the small, orn-studded doorway and I had no idea which way to turn. There were two doors besides the one through which we had entered. To the right the door opened upon the interior of the abbey tower which climbed upward with several levels that looked scarcely bigger than catwalks. This tower or series of walls rising, each higher and narrower inside the other, looked like a Babylonian ziggurat. On our left the door clearly led into larger rooms all on the level on which we stood. I wondered if the tower was in use at all. The rooms on our level, still high above the churning waters, seemed much more comfortable.

"Is Father available?" Duncan asked his brother. "We want Nell to be received in style." The bearded giant's effusiveness was charming and made things very easy for me, but I myself felt that I understood Keith Calder's cool reticence a good deal better. Gushiness made me suspicious. From my earliest girlhood, when I discovered that the Garrisons were named among the hundred richest families in America, I had found a curious ambivalence in my treatment by my friends. I gained friends who were obviously interested in what could be obtained, but I lost the friendship of some because they did not care to live in the shadow of that omnipresent dollar sign. Nor could I blame them. And now, whether I liked him or not, here, in Keith Calder, was another proud male who disliked me before there was even cause to do so, undoubtedly because of my wealth.

"You may find Freddie busy at the decanter," Keith said, apparently referring to their father, "and Emily is out somewhere rapping on walls with our Galloping Ghost Hunter. I only hope they don't stumble upon a find and ruin the artifacts."

"The abbey is valuable from an archaeological standpoint?" I asked with interest.

But it appeared that Keith did not agree with me. Perhaps he thought my question had been a polite and pointless remark made because it was expected of me.

"Valuable? Not in a dollar way that you—that others may profit by. But it is of considerable interest to an antequarian or a historian . . . Dunc, why don't you take Miss Garrison to meet Freddie? He will be delighted."

Duncan agreed with enthusiasm. "He certainly will. And why not? Father is never too old to look at beautiful blondes."

I smiled my thanks as Duncan led me off through the door on the left leading into the main living quarters of the abbey. I looked back once, saw that Keith, with my bags in his hands, was watching me. It was hard to tell what he was thinking, and I looked away quickly, embarrassed.

Duncan said, "You will notice how the monks' cells have been expanded, walls knocked out to make decent-sized rooms. Of course, the bedrooms are still in the tower."

"Really? Don't you find it difficult to heat such places? I mean the tower rooms."

He shrugged. "Never thought about it, to tell you

the truth. At all events, it wasn't our problem, thanks be! Our ancestors had to work that out. We have those little electric thing-gummies. The ones with the little stand-up white things like columns. They get all red when they're heated."

I had a vague notion of what he meant, and it gave me a very poor opinion of the heating facilities at Sea Abbey. I wondered if the sanitary arrangements were equally primitive.

"Ah! Here's Father now. What do you think of her, Father? Not quite the old moneybags you expected, eh, Sir?"

At this astonishing frankness I expected Mr. "Freddie" Calder to look shocked as we walked into the big lounge that I could see had once been a refectory for the long-dispossessed monks. But Duncan's father, a man of middle height, lines of dissipation, dyed black hair and a small, neat mustache, seemed to find nothing wrong in his son's vociferous greeting. He came to us, took my hand and squeezed it in a friendly manner I could not mistake. His eyes were a kind of muddy green, and they were the only part of him that did not seem to register delight at my arrival. He was certainly smiling and his spare body, with its slight and unexpected paunch, behaved as if he were preparing me for an immediate if gentle seduction. I found him highly amusing, which I don't think was his intention, but it was hard to dislike anyone so obvious.

"Miss Garrison!" he greeted me. "We weren't told you were such a beauty. Young Bob is like all brothers. Blind to his sister's charms." I started to say something polite, disclaiming all this flattery, but he kept on, undeterred. "What a lad he is! We've all taken him to our hearts. Miss Garrison—may I call you Elinor?—do sit down here. What are you drinking? I may tell you, Elinor, my family has become so fond of the boy, we feel as though he were our own."

"Father," Duncan reminded him with surprising presence of mind, considering his former haphazard manner, "I think Nell would like to make herself comfortable first."

"Naturally, naturally," Freddie Calder agreed promptly. He went over to a sideboard where he took up a cut glass decanter. There was no ice anywhere about; so I knew I was facing a true English family bar. "Suppose I set out a gin-and-it while you are powdering your nose or whatever. Duncan, show Elinor the—er—the powder room . . . It is just on your right as you leave the lounge."

I left my redingote and gloves in the salon and went back into the hall with Duncan.

"Used to be a sleeping cell for half a dozen monks," Duncan explained as he showed me to an attractive little bathroom whose various adornments, including a very modern electric toothbrush and water pik, could not quite disguise the severe walls and the tiny, high window.

I took time to re-do my makeup, to re-arrange and smooth my hair, and yet, when I started out into the narrow, dark hall I knew perfectly well that the man I was dressing for, Keith Calder, would not have the slightest idea that I looked any better, or any different from the wind-blown creature he had met at the dory. I snapped off the mirror light as I left the room, plunging the little hall beyond into pitch-darkness.

Suddenly, an amorphous gray creature emerged from the dark and I gasped, rigid with horror. It seemed to me that I had stepped backward in time to face one of those thousand-year-old ghostly inhabitants of the abbey.

"I beg your pardon, Madam," the ghost exclaimed in reasonably modern English. There seemed to be just a suggestion of a tremor in his voice. I could not blame the poor man. He probably thought I was a tenth-century witch.

He stumbled backward into the light of the lounge, trailing ghostly gray robes that contrasted ludicrously with his pudgy little face.

"I—I—let me introduce myself . . . Leander Rumford of the Society for Research into Psychic Phenomena."

Belatedly, I understood and apologized for my own fright. "Of course, Sir. I should have guessed immediately . . . You must have thought I was a ghost." I laughed self-consciously. "I imagine we startled each other."

The little man ushered me into the salon. "I am sure, Madam, no ghost would ever be so charming."

Freddie Calder had drinks ready. His version of gin-and-it proved to be a warm martini which I managed to get down while I listened with interest to the report of Mr. Rumford on his psychic research.

"The little bride left me in the midst of some exceedingly fine vibrations in the Second Stage Passage of the tower. Met her young man, you know."

"Are you really looking for ghostly manifestations?" I asked, wondering how they could find "psychic phenomena" in pleasant modern surroundings like this room.

The little man was shocked at the doubts I suggested.

"But yes, young lady. The ghosts of all those unhappy convicts buried in these walls."

"What!" I started up, then relaxed a little at Freddie Calder's smile.

"It happened a very long time ago, Rumford. Hardly yesterday."

Keith Calder's voice startled all three of us.

"Nevertheless, Freddie, I should think they suffered

fully as much when it happened, as they might have suffered today."

We all looked at him guiltily. His father managed to save face by remarking, "We can hardly be held accountable for the crimes of our ancestors, my dear boy. And you are shocking our guest."

"No, indeed," I ventured under Keith Calder's ironic gaze. "But I would like to know how some convicts happened to be buried in these walls."

Keith Calder took up the Scotch decanter, poured himself a drink and surprised me by coming over and standing between his father and me. I don't think Freddie Calder liked this too much. It was as if his place had been usurped, but he merely made another attempt to change the subject.

"I hope you and the others have made our Elinor's room comfortable, Keith. A room with a view. You will be impressed by the view, my dear Elinor. It was my mother's room on the third stage of the tower, but everything of hers has been removed, and Emily and Bob thought you would enjoy it because of the view. Most comfortable as well."

The dead woman's room, I thought, and glanced at Keith. This time I could not miss the friendly sympathy in his eyes. He assured me suddenly,

"A very comfortable room, Miss Garrison. And don't worry. You should not be troubled by ghosts."

Mr. Rumford began hesitantly, "I would not go so far as to say that, Sir. Manifestations of those unhappy men may appear in any walls of the—"

"Rumford," Freddie Calder cut in smoothly, "Have I showed you the latest artifacts uncovered by Keith and my boy in the foundations of the tower? Extraordinary finds, really. Shards of pottery from what may well be earlier than the tenth century."

Mr. Rumford gasped out, "Impossible! You actually believe . . . But let me see. Let me examine them. The vibrations must be truly impressive." He leaned forward anxiously as his host turned on two electric lamps at opposite ends of a display case.

While the two older men bent over the glassed-in case at the far end of the lounge, I asked Keith with a concern I tried to hide, "What is all this about convicts in the walls?" I looked around as I spoke, finding little to reassure me in a close examination of the high, arched ceiling with its ancient crossbeams whitewashed to make the room look more modern, or the double windows themselves, set deep in the huge, thick walls.

"I hadn't noticed," I added thoughtfully.

Keith seemed amused. "You hadn't noticed what?"

"How really thick these walls are."

He smiled. "They may be, but I assure you, you will find no bodies buried in them. I make no claim for the other half of the abbey, the tower and the heart of the old religious edifice, in the bedrock below the tower. Or the walls of the tower steps . . ."

"What! And you ask me to sleep there?"

He laughed. "Don't worry. We've been searching these walls for nearly ten years. If you are so lucky as to disturb some poor devil sealed up a hundred and fifty years ago, I will take him off your hands."

His amusement was contagious. "I promise you I will do precisely that," I assured him. "After I have fainted dead away."

"I doubt it, Miss Garrison. You look fragile but I don't think you are."

I said doubtfully, as I finished my revolting drink, "I'm not at all sure that is a compliment."

"I did not say it was."

That put me in my place. I tried to retain a degree of coolness, an indifference that served me well in other situations, but how can one use these qualities against a man who has them ahead of you? I recovered my outward poise, though a certain inner calm was badly shaken.

"But this isn't telling me about your uninvited guests sealed in the walls, Mr. Calder."

"True. Now, you will want to supervise Mrs. Milligan's unpacking. I suggest we discuss these convicts while I show you your tower room. You will find it inspiring, built upon endless skeletal remains, as we suppose."

"Good heavens! That will be inspiring to what? Mr. Rumford's ghosts?" Then, appreciating the absurdity of this conversation and his deliberate effort to arouse me, I laughed and agreed that I would like to see to my unpacking. "But no ghostly manifestations."

He took my arm, helped me to my feet. "I promise if anything manifests—is that what they do?—I'll call in Leander. But just now he seems more interested in that crushed chalice I found on the lower level some days ago. Come along."

He seemed to be the kind of man who would not accept a refusal; so I went along obediently. In the doorway we were briefly stopped by Freddie Calder.

"Elinor, my dear, may I whip up another gin-and-it for you?"

"Thank you, but not right now."

Keith guessed my anxious attempt to escape and I knew from the crinkle of amusement around his eyes that he also guessed why.

"Freddie, I am going to show Miss Garrison around the abbey. Dinner at eight?"

At first I thought Freddie Calder did not want us wandering around the abbey, but the older man's curious objection made me wonder if it wasn't my escort—his illegitimate son—he really objected to.

"That won't be necessary, Old Boy. Leave Elinor to me. Have another drink, Elinor, and I'll be with you in just a jiff."

"Later, Freddie," his son told him decisively. "Later."

"But Keith, I wanted to see to Elinor's—"

Abrupt as Keith was with his father, I found myself relieved to be politely avoiding the older man, though I was careful not to let Keith guess. I felt that there might be more filial affection here than they demonstrated before strangers. The hall was still dark when we started back toward the high-walled little courtyard through which we had entered the modern part of the abbey, and I clutched Keith Calder anxiously, letting him lead me wherever he chose.

"Aren't there any lights?"

"We manage with our own little power plant. Not very reliable, I'm afraid. The romance of Sea Abbey is fairly well known, but the realism is something else again."

"I hope you invest heavily in candles."

"To the limit." He startled me by practically lifting me over and around a suitcase that someone had dropped in the middle of the hall. We had passed several closed doors and I thought whoever owned the suitcase and had carelessly left it in our way, must be behind one of those narrow doors. Our way was now dimly lighted from somewhere in the courtyard ahead.

"Were they all monks' cells in the good old days?" I asked curiously. "Very small rooms, aren't they?"

He did not glance in their direction, but I had an idea he was angry about the suitcase. He kicked it aside impatiently.

"I don't know how good those old days were, but Henry the Eighth changed their plans. The Calders were awarded this abbey for their services to the Crown at the time of the dissolution of the monasteries. The Calders obliged Henry with some favors, I believe."

"In what way?"

"They were highly successful pimps, probably."

I laughed. He was nothing if not frank. "Then it wasn't those dispossessed monks who left that suitcase for us to stumble over."

"That?" We stepped out into the courtyard with its strange, high-laced white globe lights that gave an eery, almost ghostly look to our faces and our lengthening shadows. "No. The suitcase belongs to Duncan's wife."

"Duncan's wife!" The friendly, bearded young giant seemed the last man in the world to be married. The irritating thing about Keith Calder was his ability to read my mind.

"He doesn't look the married type . . . Wasn't that what you were going to say? They all do."

"*They*—who?"

He grinned. "Everyone who meets him. But Bessie will assure you that he is very much married." He glanced back at the suitcase. "She has been in Bristol over the weekend, shopping. She is a very rich young lady."

I thought of the rough channel waters, the wind slapping our faces, and I did not envy Bessie Calder her voyage across from the Abbeyvue harbor in the darkness.

Keith and I had just reached the easterly door into the tower and the most ancient sector of the abbey when we heard a screech which I took to be that of some wild tropic bird, an unpleasant and probably predatory bird.

"What in heaven's name was that?"

"That would be Bessie," he said, with a quickly concealed grimace.

Astonished and with a strong desire to laugh, I swung around. Keith was a little slower, sighing. I saw something like a huge yellow bird emerge from the darkness of the hall we had just left. The bird proved to be Bessie Calder, a plump, youngish woman in spite of the harsh whiteness of what I took to be a wig and the huge, pale blob of her lipstick.

"Dunc! Don't you lay hands on that Yank hussy! If anybody's going to marry all that money, it's . . . Oh, God! Is that you, Keith?"

"None other, Bess. Did you enjoy yourself in Bristol?"

"What's to do in Bristol, me-laddie? Say, introduce me to the Yank and I'll apologize to her in style."

Only Keith's friendly warning nudge helped me to recover my sober manners as we met her. Keith made the introductions, Mrs. Calder and I shook hands, and Bessie looked me over, pursing her shiny lips critically. While I stood there self-consciously trying to think of something trivial that would fit this occasion, Keith started to maneuver me away, saying, "Later, Bess. Miss Garrison hasn't seen her room yet, and she wants to change for dinner."

Bessie caught my sleeve with blood-colored nails whose length impressed me. Her alcoholic breath was equally impressive.

"Miss Garrison, tell me. I know this laddie won't. Which of them is making a play for you? Keith or Freddie?"

I started to say "neither," realized this was merely catering to her nasty inquisitiveness, and fumbled with an "I've no idea" while Keith said warningly, "Bess!"

She leaned closer to me. "You mustn't let it crunch you, but it happened to me."

"Bess, for God's sake! Shall we go, Miss Garrison?"

I think it was Keith's impatience that aroused my curiosity.

"I don't think I understand, Mrs. Calder. What happened to you?"

"I thought it—" She licked her lips, started again. "I thought it was love. But it was my money. That's to—to say . . . Pa's money. Made it with a little private club in old Lunnon. Gambling. And now they'd love to get rid of me. But if he divorces me, they won't have my nice new pound notes. Shocked?"

"Not at all," I said pleasantly. "My great-grandfather gambled all the way around the Horn. Shall we go, Mr. Calder?"

Neither of us said anything until we had gone into the gloomy tower half of the abbey. I could hardly find my way along the stone passage until Keith surprised me by snapping on a series of dim light bulbs so small I thought privately they would serve to light a toy Christmas tree.

"As I said, the power plant is somewhat inadequate."

It was no use. I kept returning in my thoughts to Bessie Calder's warning. As Keith turned me away from the long, dark, lower passage toward a well-worn flight of stone steps leading upward into more darkness, I said suddenly, "I wonder if there was any truth in Mrs. Calder's remark."

He did not hesitate. "If you mean that my father would like to marry you for your fortune, I've no doubt our Bess is right. Freddie Calder's life style requires expensive supplemental interest."

. . . And after a marriage for money? Was Bessie Calder right about that, too? That they—surely not friendly Duncan!—wanted to get rid of her and keep her fortune? But there was only one way to be sure, absolutely sure!

"Are you cold?" Keith asked.

"No. Not yet, at any rate."

"But you shivered."

"No," I said. "That was a shudder."

I hoped he did not understand me.

THREE

The steps led upward in one direction to a landing that was sufficiently wide to give me hopes for the rest of the square tower. These hopes were eventually dashed as the steps grew narrower and more sloping, the stone itself worn away toward the inner wall until it reminded me of that harrowing level at the top of the Leaning Tower of Pisa. Despite the occasional electric light set into a niche in the inner wall, with the electric cord itself snaking its way upward along the same wall, I felt that I had stumbled into an instant horror movie.

Some of the steps were so worn and slippery I clutched projecting stone edges while, behind me, Keith reached out to lend me a hand.

"Careful, Miss Garrison. You may have just uncovered one of our former, and unwilling, inhabitants."

My groping fingers leaped off the wall as though it had scorched me. Trying to cover my absurd reaction, I reminded him, more nonchalantly than I felt, "You haven't yet told me what your convict friends are doing in the walls.

We reached the first stage of the tower where a narrow, heavy door, Keith told me, would lead us to the bedrooms of most of the family.

"All but Bess. She refuses to sleep here at all."

"Ghosts?"

He promised me, "I really will tell you all about

those poor convict devils, but I thought if we treated the matter as a joke, we might persuade you that you will enjoy my grandmother's tower apartment, in spite of my sister-in-law's dislike of the place."

I stopped with one foot on the step above.

"Oh! And is that why Mrs. Calder has her room in the modern half of the abbey?"

"I'm afraid it is. Bess has a powerful imagination. As you heard."

I had it on the tip of my tongue to ask, "Was it all imagination?" But I said nothing about Bess Calder, even though I privately suspected she was nearer right about my popularity at Sea Abbey than I had originally wanted to admit. Certainly, the Calders showed Bess no respect, having perhaps bled her of her father's fortune. It was something to remember when I found Keith Calder or Duncan Calder a little too fascinating. I wondered if my brother Bob had any notion of these other currents at Sea Abbey. It was also impossible to forget that there had been discussion between Bob and Duncan about new boats, et cetera, that the Calders would receive after the wedding of Bob and Emily Calder. Clearly, the Calders expected to profit by the marriage with one of the dollar-rich Garrisons.

"Where is my brother's room?" I asked as we neared the second narrow, iron-bound door which I supposed must open upon the tower apartment once occupied by the grandmother of the Calders who—somehow—fell out of a window and died.

Keith opened the door into a narrow passage, so narrow, in fact, that I made a joke about walking sideways, and Keith, keeping up the joke, admitted it was fortunate I was so slim. I accepted this little compliment with the properly light spirit, and when we passed a closed door, I inquired if this was my room—where his grandmother had died.

"No. This is Emily's apartment. Granny's—that is, yours, faces the west . . . Here we are."

I looked back. "How is Emily? Shouldn't we have seen her before now? I am naturally anxious to meet my future sister-in-law."

He hesitated with his hand on the doorknob of the tower room where his grandmother had fallen to her death.

"Emily and your brother had a little ritual they were going to perform today. Her unexpected illness postponed it, but I imagine that is why they disappeared. It was meant to be only a few minutes. They meant to make their marriage vows before the abbey altar. That is at the end of the passage on the main floor."

I remembered the long, dark, tunnel-like hall that we had avoided in order to take the steps up to our present high eminence. The more I heard about the Sea Abbey of the Calders, the less I liked the sound of it.

It was another matter when we entered the room assigned to me. Small but comfortable, with a tasteful choice of furnishings including an extraordinarily comfortable four-poster bed whose mattress Keith tested for me with one fist, the room invited me and I said so. He nodded, pleased.

"Emily was sure you would like it. Some of us thought you might prefer more elegance. More—"

"I'm afraid you didn't know me very well," I reminded him, trying to say it lightly. "Did Bob give you that impression of me?"

He looked at me for a long moment. I was sensitive to his opinion and slightly hurt that he should have such a bad picture of a woman he didn't even know. He himself brought up with a smile that softened all his features.

"I did not know you then. You must forgive me.

And Bob didn't quite do justice to you, though I will admit he was generous, for a mere brother. But you see, the absence of money gives curious values to people like the Calders, and Bob's view of you was overruled. You remained only a very rich woman, with a rich woman's tastes."

"Not for the first time," I said cynically. But my two Gucci cases were here. The housekeeper had already unpacked for me and snapped on the warm, glowing lamp at one side of the dressing table. I felt at home here in this room as I had not felt in a long time, including my newly redecorated Fifth Avenue apartment back in New York.

Keith Calder had gone to the long window that opened upon a tiny terrace. He unfastened the modern French window.

"Fairly cold, but you may enjoy the view."

I came up behind him, gasped at the crenellated rooftops of the abbey's western half, and then, beyond it, at the glittering night waters of the channel which was still busy with boats. Fishing boats, I thought, and smallish craft of varying sizes, occasionally an impressively larger ship, all going about their work. The sky above was so dark it was hard to tell where the sky ended and the channel began. There were lights along the shore. Abbeyvue and beyond, probably.

"You were right," I said. "I love it. What a fabulous view! Your grandmother chose this room? I admire her taste." Then I remembered the ominous aspect of the tower apartment. "You will probably think this demonstrates my appalling bad taste, but can you tell me where your grandmother—how she died?"

"Perfectly understandable." He sounded sincere. He pushed the door open wide and pointed to the low crenellated stone wall about three feet high. The little terrace itself was less than a yard wide, but it ran around three sides of the tower. My knees shook as I looked down to the courtyard an endless distance below, barely visible in all its light and shadow, thanks to a gathering fog and the faintness of the light within those thick, misty globes.

He took my arm, more gently this time. "Not too close. We don't want to repeat that horror."

"Did anyone see her fall?" The entire story of the old lady's fall was horrible, but like many intimate horrors, it aroused deep curiosity.

"Emily was in the courtyard below. She was nearly struck by her grandmother's body. An added touch of the macabre. We were . . . bitter about it for some time."

"I should think so," I said, looking away from the ghastly scene. "I think I had better wash and dress for dinner. Do the ladies dress?"

"I suppose you would call them cocktail dresses. They aren't quite in my province. The bathroom, by the way, is through that door below the bed. To your left." He paused in the doorway to the little, dark passage and looked me over. I wondered what he was thinking. He said suddenly, "It was good of you to come, Miss Garrison. I hope we don't frighten you away." Then the door closed. He was gone.

I set about placing my articles of makeup in new arrangements on the dressing table near the long French door which acted as the only window in the room. There was a pink, cheerful glow from the lamp on the dressing table. It had a good effect on my nerves, soothing my doubts, reminding me of the warm comforts in this room. As for the other—the death of that old lady—I would not think of that.

But it was difficult to avoid it.

I washed and dressed in a knee-length black sheath with only a fun necklace to give it color, and I sat down to renew my makeup, to give my own face more color, and there, before me, was the long French door, and the wall beyond, and I could not, after all, forget the lady who had died. Small wonder that Bess Calder had refused to stay in this room!

I did not know quite what to make of Bess. Because I had been inclined to dislike her at once, I felt an odd, perverse sense that she might be telling me the truth. Perhaps she had been married for her money, that the Calders would like very much to keep the money and rid themselves of Bess, and that there might be the same plans involving me. But not, surely, from Keith Calder!

I was putting the finishing touches to my mascara, peering intently into the mirror, when I was startled to see a movement in the reflection that was not my own. The movement had been the door opening, of course. A remarkably gingerly operation for such a simple matter. I waited without turning around. I restrained my first annoyed impulse to jump up and throw the door open.

More Calder attempts to put me in my dollar-grubby place, or to scare me away, for some obscure reason?

The passage beyond was so dark the door was half open before I made out the figure. About that time a coltish young head of uncombed hair appeared around the door. This apparition could also make noises, unmistakably teen-aged giggles stifled with difficulty. I did not turn around but spoke to the mirrored reflection, softening my voice with a smile.

"Come in, Ghost of Sea Abbey. I've been anxious to meet you."

Emily Calder slapped the door with girlish impatience.

"You knew all the time."

"Not quite all the time." I got up and started across

the room. She came in, loped toward me in her leggy, coltish and altogether charming way. She was wearing a too-long, unbecoming tan cardigan sweater and a mini-skirt that had seen better days. Behind her, Bob stepped into the room, proudly watching the endearing if childish antics of his fiancee. I thought she was going to throw her arms around me and I offered my arms, ready to hug her, but a little to my chagrin, she took my arms and held me off, looking me up and down.

"Isn't she marvy, Bobbin? You could tell at once she's chic as a Yankee dollar. The way she dresses, walks, looks . . . You're everything you should be, Miss Garrison. Isn't she, Bobbin?"

I put the best face I could put on this dubious greeting, especially as I saw that Bob found nothing wrong or unpleasant in her words about "Yankee dollars."

"Not bad for a sister." Bob took my hand and Emily's and joined them. "Please like each other, my two favorite people."

"We do that already," I assured him and kissed Emily's cool cheek.

Emily giggled. "You see, Bobbin? She likes me already. Nell . . . I shall call you Nell, exactly like Bob . . . how do you like this room? We tried to make it warm and cozy."

"I love it. Charming," I said.

Bob was obviously relieved. "I knew you would. At first, Emy and I debated about whether you mightn't like it because of . . ."

". . . what happened here," Emily finished. Bob glanced at her anxiously and I thought there was a kind of stiff bravado in her young face. "They probably told you about Granny; so we'll just leave it at that."

"It is a lovely room," I told her. "Worthy of a

lovely person. I wish I had known your grandmother."

"Thank you, Nell. Oh—Bobbin!" The girl hugged him, bubbling with her young enthusiasm. "She's even nicer than you promised, and she doesn't act her age at all, thank God!"

I cringed inwardly at this remark about my age, but put the best possible face on it and suggested to Bob, "Shall we start down to dinner now?"

"Of course. I'm sorry. Emy, stop rattling. Let's get going." He took his fiancee's arm and mine and started toward the door. He had no difficulty with me, but Emily was embarrassingly busy over my clothes hung up by the housekeeper in the clothespress standing in the corner beside the door.

"Darling! Wait a sec. Oh, it's glorious to be rich. Nell, did you get all these in Paris? This is a Cardin, isn't it? And another—No! A Dior?"

"Givenchy," I said, uncomfortable at her overwhelming manner and wondering how I might make it possible for young Emily to acquire a wardrobe of Paris fashions without making it seem like a bribe or a vulgar gift from one of those Yankee dollar females.

And there had been talk of money again! I remembered Bessie's accusation. It began to seem that Bess Calder understood her in-laws much better than Bob did.

"Forget it, Sweetheart," Bob told Emily goodnaturedly. "Once you're Mrs. Robert Garrison, you can have all the Givenchy's, or whatever, that your little heart desires."

"Darling! Darling! I wish I could marry you tonight." Her feverish enthusiasm made me recall suddenly that she had been sick this morning. Perhaps that would explain this excess of energy now.

I felt frightfully guilty, like a wicked mother-in-law, when my brother's promise and her acceptance gave me a twinge of dismay. Heaven knew Bob's wife had as much right to a beautiful wardrobe as I had! I should credit young Emily with full honors for honesty. Bob could never say she had not been frank.

As we made our way along the passage toward the steps, I remembered Emily's own room was on this level of the tower.

"When you two are married," I said after searching for a harmless pleasantry about their future, "you will probably live in the highest penthouse in Europe . . . judging by this tower."

I couldn't have chosen a happier subject. Emily clutched my hand across Bob's body.

"You are a dear! That's exactly where we'll live; won't we, Bobbin? On top of the Eiffel Tower . . . or at least high enough to look down on old Eiffel. Not to mention Buckingham Palace."

We all laughed and then started down the stone steps in single file, Bob leading the way and Emily behind me.

"The lights are pretty scarce," Bob apologized. "The power plant here on the island is kind of like a toy. You never know how reliable it's going to be."

Emily put in cheerfully, "But there are candles and matches everywhere. Look along the outer wall. You will see a little niche every few yards. If you put your hand in, even in the dark, you will find matches and a candlestick. Rather an adventure, I always think; don't you?"

I agreed that such adventures were delightful and added the slight untruth that the reliability of the power did not in the least bother me. Then, as I reached out to test her advice about the niches full of candles and matches, I thought of that absurd tale about sealed-in convicts, with which Keith Calder had regaled me earlier.

Finding, as Emily had promised, that there really were matches and a candlestick in the first niche, I ran my fingers along the rough stone blocks, remarking as casually as I could, "Is there actually someone sealed up in one of these walls?"

In front of me Bob stopped suddenly. "Good Lord, Nell! Who's been feeding you those horror stories?"

"Then it isn't true?" But it seemed odd that a man like Keith should have frightened me with such a fantastic lie.

Emily, who had run into me when we stopped so unexpectedly, said in a quick, impatient voice, "It's not exactly a secret. You might as well know, Nell. We've even got a psychic ghost hunter in the place now, testing for the poor fellows. Actually, we Calders think it gives a kind of glamor to the Old Home Place."

"You mean someone is buried in the walls of the abbey?"

Bob turned and looked up at us. "As I understand it, the thing happened back in the eighteenth century; so the modern Calders feel it gives an added historic interest to the place. The Calder of that day was a sailing man. He made a contract to carry convicted men out of England, presumably to Botany Bay. Since they were virtually his property, he simply had them taken to the island here, to rebuild the abbey, which was going to rack and ruin."

"Well," Emily put in, reasonably, "they really were our property, though I admit he shouldn't have done what he did."

I asked, "What did he do?"

"The authorities found out, but Calder was warned in time; so he had the troublemakers among the convicts sealed behind the new walls."

"My God! Then it is true!"

Before Bob could express an opinion, Emily reminded me, "It was an awfully long time ago." She added in a small, scared voice, "I hope you won't hold it against my family. They—they wouldn't do a thing like that today."

I was forced to laugh at that, an absurd end to a grisly tale, but Bob, for some reason, was annoyed either by my flippant attitude or his fiancee's defensiveness.

"Don't be an idiot, Emy! Nobody's accusing you of anything . . . And Nell, it's not funny, sealing people up in walls, convicts or not."

Nobody said anything for a few minutes. We went on down the steps, past the door to the first level, and on to the courtyard level, but nobody touched the walls again. We met Duncan Calder and Bessie in the courtyard. They were arguing, at least Bessie was arguing. Her big husband was pleading with her to lower her voice.

"I tell you, sweetheart, I never touched it. You must have made a mistake in the account. I haven't even been in Bristol now for weeks."

"You were in Bath only last Saturday, and it's not very far from Bath to the Bristol Bank. In fact, why couldn't you have dealt with Barclays' branch in Bath?"

"Hush, Sweetheart! You can't have forgotten already that ruffled thing-gummy I brought back for you to wear while you loll around that damned room of yours."

"Loll around! You never enter it. How would you know?"

I am not certain what Emily's and Bob's reactions were, but my own was one of acute discomfort at overhearing this intimate conjugal argument which was none of my business. I stepped back into the tower's main passage, scraping my shoe sole on the uneven stone in the hope that it would arouse the Calders to our presence.

Bob was more direct. "Hey, kids! Time for dinner. You can argue on your own time."

Duncan laughed as Emily did, and he threw his hands up in surrender, but his wife's round face remained sullen and unhappy in the ugly white light of the globe over her head which also threw her white-blonde wig into harsh relief. Emily went up to her brother, took his hand and tugged him toward the hall in the more modern half of the abbey. This left the unhappy Bessie alone and Bob and I joined her as unobtrusively as possible.

"I don't know about you," he said brightly, "but I'm starved. I could eat one of those stuffed boar's heads they used to serve in these places."

I said, "Me too." I began to rattle on about not having stopped for lunch since leaving London, and other pointless details, but, at least, Bessie perked up a little, borrowed Bob's handkerchief, and went along with us. She asked me,

"Ever been to Bristol? I just got back myself."

"No. I've always wanted to see Bath, which I understand is nearby."

"Yeah. And they've got a Barclays' Bank in Bath, too. A branch, that is."

Remembering her argument with her husband over money and the Bristol and Bath matters, I was sorry I had brought back a painful subject to her. I started to change the subject but Bessie beat me to it. She looked me over as she pointed to the double doors on the right of the hall.

"There we are. It used to be some sort of church interior. But when the Calders took over ages ago, they put a table where the pews were, and a sideboard where the altar used to be. A bit of all right! For the Calders. Always seemed kind of sacrilegious to me."

With surprising anger Bob said abruptly, "That

happened over three hundred years ago, kindly remember."

Bessie and I exchanged astonished glances. Bessie came back with the very American, "So what?" But I could see that my brother was obviously worried over the reputation of the Calder family. The more I heard about them, the more I felt he had cause to worry. It was quite true that it was none of my business. I wasn't marrying a Calder. Nonetheless, the place itself, even more than the family, was beginning to get to me. The longer I remained here the more I felt the unhappiness and pain and horror of past centuries creeping into my bones.

And then Freddie Calder called out to us from the fabulous high-roofed, long room that was the dining hall of Sea Abbey.

"There you are. We've been waiting for our guest of honor. Come in, Elinor. Do come in." And he followed this by arriving in the doorway almost on a run. I was keenly aware of Keith Calder's shadowy presence behind his father. He said nothing but he was watching me with great intensity. Almost, I thought with outrage, as though he and the Calders were passing judgment on my fitness to be an in-law of the family.

But by the time Duncan had ushered me to the chair on the right of his father, I was secretly amused at my own pride. Hadn't I come to Sea Abbey with more or less the same idea—to place my stamp of approval on the Calder family?

And my first dinner at the Calder table was nothing if not interesting. Everyone seemed to be on his best behavior, including the married pair, Bessie and Duncan, and I found the relationship between Bob and Emily tender and charming. She deferred to him in a youthful, endearing way, and he was masterful, caring for her, arranging her napkin, seeing to it that her chair was moved closer to the table, chiding her that she must only eat things that agreed with her: "Emy isn't going to be sick again if I have to test everything before she eats it."

"Wow!" Bessie cut in loudly. "A body'd think you was afraid she'd be poisoned."

Duncan laughed. "Not surprising, when one considers the meat they sell us these days."

"That's not what Bess had in mind," Emily giggled into her napkin.

Everybody looked at her. Bob reached for her hand and squeezed it. I wondered if he was trying to warn her to be discreet, and that, naturally, led me to wonder if there was something sinister about Emily's upset stomach. It was absurdly melodramatic, but then, Sea Abbey was a study in melodrama. And Emily lived up to my worst suspicions: "But it's simple! Something I ate was poisoned. Somebody doesn't like me." She slapped away Bob's warning hand. "I was poisoned for my fabulous fortune!" and she burst into laughter.

It was only very belatedly that we all joined in and found humor in the remark of a penniless girl.

FOUR

Fortunately for the success of the Calders' dinner, Emily's outrageous remark was accepted as an amusing addition to the party. The subject moved on to politics, even more absurd, and I was a good deal surprised to discover that it was eleven o'clock when we left the great chamber with its high crossbeams and long windows, the latter an obvious replacement in clear glass and drapes for the original stained glass that had once illuminated an altar.

Freddie Calder insisted on escorting me to my little tower apartment. I had thought of getting to know Emily better on our way up to our crow's nest rooms, but I was touched to see the girl go off to walk lovingly, arm in arm, with Bob out through the narrow archway to the stone steps by which we had entered Sea Abbey. I was so carried away by this indication of their love that I found myself jarred by Keith's sharp reminder to the lovers.

"Take care. Those steps are slippery at this hour. There's a heavy mist off the channel."

Emily called back as she swung Bob's hand in an endearingly childish way. "Don't be tiresome, Keith. Weren't you ever in love? Everything's smooth when you're in love. Try it some time."

Freddie was rather too closely urging me across the courtyard, and I started along obediently, dying to look back at Keith, but my view was obstructed by Keith's father.

"He wouldn't do for you at all, my dear Elinor," Freddie assured me with the suave conviction of a man who knows all about women's needs.

I couldn't resist asking, "In what way, Mr. Calder?"

"Freddie."

"Freddie . . . You must know me very well to be so sure of my tastes."

"A woman of your sophistication? No. It is the only possible reason you are still *Miss* Garrison at—" He broke off, but the rest of his sentence was obvious.

. . . at your age.

"The least you can do is call me *Ms*.," I said, playing it lightly. As we stepped into the passage of the old tower, I noted that Keith Calder had turned and gone back into the modern half of the abbey. I felt a sudden resentment at the suggestion that there must be something wrong with me because I wasn't married at thirty-one, and I should therefore be anxious to marry Keith or Freddie or almost anyone who would have me. After all, I had been engaged long ago and but for the tragedy of Stephen's death in the helicopter crash, I would be an old married woman now.

"It is still early," Freddie reminded me as we reached the beginning of the tower steps. "Let me show you the oldest part of the abbey where the original altar and nave remain. Leander Rumford has been doing some work in here, and he considers it very promising."

"Heavens!" I said. I'd forgotten him entirely. "Does he spend all his time digging rather than eating with the rest of you?"

"Far from it. But he is jealous of the work being done by my sons. He feels that they may accidentally uncover some of his spooks while they are looking for pottery and other relics of an unpleasant past. So he takes his dinner early, in his room, and hangs about in these dungeons sounding for ghosts while we dine like civilized men."

"I don't envy him," I said. Nothing looked less inviting than that dark, cave-like hole leading to what must surely be the coldest, dreariest church interior in England. I tried to make excuses.

"I really am rather tired, I think I will turn in, if you don't mind."

"Oh, but I do. Come now, Elinor. You aren't that old, surely!"

Of course that did it. I couldn't let this man twenty years my senior accuse me of being old. I shrugged.

"Well, then, let's be on our way. How far is it?"

"Marvelous wine cellar, unless Leander has drunk it all to keep warm," he joked. "Don't give a thought to the cold. I've some brandy tucked away in there that I promise you will restore the sparkle to those pretty eyes and a tingle to your toes."

In Freddie Calder's company this hardly sounded tempting, but I could not turn back now without insulting the poor man, and I could tell by his manner, and a certain long-established arrogance, that he believed himself irresistible. I found myself hoping our gloomy excursion into this rocky tomb would be interrupted by the presence of that tireless ghost hunter, Leander Rumford.

We passed beyond the steps. By the light of one of those mini globes along the wall of the main passage, I saw a small, damp recess that opened out of the passage and ended behind the steps. Because I preferred not to be the first along that passage into the heart of the abbey, I stepped aside, my shoe scraping on the rough, wet stone. It was rougher than I had expected and I nearly fell. Before Freddie could reach out to catch me, I saved myself by flattening my hand against the wall. I let out a cry that was more of a yelp.

"Ugh! It—it moved under my fingers!" It was so sickening I lurched forward, into Freddie Calder's waiting arms. He grinned. His mustache twitched.

"Lucky lichen!"

"What!"

With his arms still uncomfortably tight around me, he swung me around.

"You see? Just mould and lichen growing where the moisture seeps through."

It may have been the eery light or my imagination, but patches of that loathsome growth looked like watery blood, to my eyes. I stammered, "The—the color . . . like blood. Oh, it must be my imagination."

"Not at all," Freddie assured me with pride. "It's exactly this sort of thing old Leander plays with. My boys don't like him hanging about here, but I gave him permission because he may find something valuable. Never know. Besides, he and the Society pay me for his board and room here at the abbey. He makes all sorts of claims. Ghosts to the right and ghosts to the left. Tell me, my dear, do you feel the psychic bonds enclosing you?"

I felt some bonds enclosing me but there was nothing psychic about them. I tried to release myself without offending him. It was not easy. In the end I had to resort to trickery by looking surprised amd murmuring, "Why, it's Mr. Rumford; isn't it?" And then, as Freddie let me go, I rubbed my arms, pretending it was my reaction to the cold.

Freddie stepped ahead of me into the passage, peering around. "I only hope you didn't see one of Leander's ghostly friends by mistake. Where the devil—? Doesn't seem to be here now. Leander!" His raised voice echoed through the passage and seemed to be swallowed in some great, hollow space beyond. "Are you here, old man?"

Dimly, as if from the caverns of the earth, the little psychic researcher answered us. "Here, my boy! Behind the altar. Marvelous vibrations. Lamp keeps fading. Come along, I say!"

Freddie called out, "Trouble?" as we moved along the passage.

"Dashed lantern dimmed! Either manifestations or . . . Oh—oh, drat! Only the wind blowing through these crevices."

Freddie and I both laughed. It was an enormous relief to me, and after that, I was able to walk along between those damp, foul-smelling walls with what would pass reasonably well for enthusiasm.

"Here we are," Freddie warned me. "Take care. As we enter the nave, it gets rough underfoot. Some fifty years ago the flooring—all the slabs of stone across the entrance—were torn up. I'm afraid they were rather carelessly replaced."

I walked carefully, remarking with pseudo good cheer, "Looking for bodies, were they?"

"No. More practical. Searching for old treasures of the abbey, concealed when the monasteries were secularized. Jewelled chalices . . . gold and silver ewers . . . the usual things. But the Calders never had much luck after the Tudor period. Nothing of any value was discovered, though the antequarians went mad over the trash they found. Antequarians! Poor idiots like my boy Keith."

Although I, personally, had never thought much about old goblets and the signs of other civilizations, I did admire those people who understood and cared about such things. I felt a deeper admiration for Keith with his antequarian interest, than for those Calders grubbing frantically for the treasures of long-dead monks.

At the entrance to what must have been the original nave of the abbey church, the electric line ended. From here onward the lighting depended upon lanterns carried by the visitors. From the dim light of Leander Rumford's lantern behind the altar at the far end of the church interior, Freddie found enough illumination to light a big oil lantern. Besides the lantern, in a niche where devotion candles may once have been sold, there was a useful-looking, outsized flashlight. I took it up, not intending to be caught again in the dark with only fungus for company. Thus suitably armed, I followed Freddie. If I had possessed enough courage, I would have walked right back out through that cold passage and up to my room instead of tagging along through this clammy tomb.

"You see the glass behind the altar?" Freddie pointed out. "Stained glass half a millennium in age—almost all destroyed during the bombings. When I heard about it, I hoped it might uncover something. Treasure, you know. But no luck, as usual."

He was getting too far ahead of me and there were too many odd sounds like the echo of footsteps surrounding me, which, oftener than not, proved to be moisture seeping out of the walls and down upon the worn rock below. I called to Freddie in sudden fright. "Mr. Calder—Freddie! This is no place to be caught alone."

"Sorry." He came back for me, his muddy green eyes sparkling in the light of lantern and flashlight. "Missed me, eh, Nell?" He gave me a squeeze that nearly took my breath away. I was almost sorry he had come back for me. "Now, we'll fetch up that brandy, and have a little nightcap. Shall we invite poor old Leander?"

"Please do!" Definitely. Anyone. "And then I really

would like to go back. It was a long drive today, and I am a little tired."

The jolly, pudgy little face of Leander Rumford popped up from a frightful hole behind the altar. "Do I hear my name called? Brr! Slightly dampish in here. I should welcome that spot of brandy." He came around what remained of the altar, a huge block of stone, with the solid, eternal look of Stonehenge, and a gigantic crucifix of some greenish metal precariously balanced on a wooden block.

"One minute," Freddie promised, "and I'll have that brandy." He left me with Leander while he retraced our steps through the nave of the great, hollow edifice that had once been virtually an underground church. With its enormous, dark space, its endless corners as secret as the grave, and smelling much the same, this heart of the abbey filled me with a peculiar horror that was half fascination. Freddie set his lantern down on the uneven floor and began to feel around behind the stone shelf where the thin tapers had once gleamed. Gradually, he seemed to dissolve into the great dark.

Leander extended his hands. "I wonder if I dare ask you?" His fingers were stiff with cold. I took the lantern from him and set it down. I rubbed his crabbed hands vigorously. First, he winced, as the circulation returned. Then his smile came back. His little eyeballs rolled nervously.

"You hear that?"

I listened. Somewhere, water dropped upon stone in even little splashes.

"No, no. Visitants. The ancient monks who carved this great edifice out of rock and earth; it is like footsteps."

It certainly sounded like faint movements somewhere near. We were kneeling in the heavy shadow under what remained of the great altar. I moved to see if Freddie Calder was returning. There was a rush of icy air and above my head something huge and black seemed to hover momentarily before it tumbled over, missing my head by mere inches.

I screamed, but I had scrambled back on top of poor Mr. Rumford so rapidly that the falling crucifix merely tore my sleeve and carved a deep scratch in my arm as it passed me, crashing upon earth and over-turned stone. The sound of that metal on stone echoed in waves through the nave, bringing running footsteps and Freddie Calder waving a brandy bottle.

"What the devil! Is anyone hurt? Good God! How could that have happened?"

"My lantern . . ." Rumford cried plaintively, feeling around with one hand.

"May I *please* go to my room, Mr. Calder?" I was shaking so much I found it difficult to get to my feet. Freddie Calder, murmuring inanities about the low incidence of such accidents, helped me up.

"A small brandy? Just a wee dram? It's rather a tiring walk back to the steps and up to your room. And unfortunately, there are no lifts at Sea Abbey."

"Never mind the brandy. Or the lifts. Just point me in the right direction and I'll go by myself."

"You know, Mr. Calder," Leander Rumford put in with sudden new interest, "we may have uncovered some rare vibrations with the fall of that crucifix. The whole thing may even have been contrived by one of our spirit friends. Most promising."

Grabbing the big flashlight which had rolled half-way across the nave, I started the length of this ancient church, reflecting that there had been no side-alleys, so I could hardly get lost. I might break my neck, but I would, at least, know where I was when I broke my neck.

Freddie, meanwhile, was trying to persuade the psychic researcher to leave as well.

"Hadn't you better come along, old boy. You can contact your spirits tomorrow in the daylight."

"My dear Calder, it will never be daylight down here. And the fall of that crucifix was definitely a message to me."

"It was a message to me, to get out of here," I called angrily.

"Very possible," said Leander, taking all this with high seriousness. "Dear Miss Garrison, you are allowing a selfish concern for your safety to outweigh all the benefits of psychic discovery . . . However, it is quite chilly in here. I believe I might be forgiven a few hours' sleep."

"Good," Freddie said. "Come along with us."

I had already started when Mr. Rumford joined Freddie. "Quite a lucky thing all around, the fall of that great crucifix. It was a sign to me. Don't let anyone raise it until I get back here tomorrow."

I grumbled, "And kindly tell your spirits not to knock strangers on the head when they want to deliver messages to you."

Mr. Rumford, his feelings hurt, subsided into silence, but Freddie Calder laughed at my fuss over what he called "a simple accident." Ashamed of my outburst, I made no more protests. My arm was beginning to sting and smart, and my sleeve was a complete mess, but I was still a little dazed by the whole episode. There were moments during that tiresome walk over the uneven, sunken blocks of stone when I felt that it had all been a series of little nightmares. It was silly, and I had not been seriously hurt, but my nerves were playing me tricks. Probably because this place was as close to a grave as I wanted to find myself for some years ahead.

After all his warnings to me, Freddie Calder stumbled over that badly dug and reburied area in front of the church interior. Mr. Rumford and I each took one of his arms and got him up. But contrary to my own bad example, he did not lose his temper. We were still in the passage leading past the tower steps when a totally unexpected figure came hurrying toward us. I was still in a state where I half expected this to be one of Mr. Rumford's ghostly manifestations, but the running figure suddenly flashed a light in our faces and we saw the damp, rocky walls, the oppressive and jagged rock ceiling overhead, and Keith Calder behind the light.

"I heard a terrific crash. Freddie, what the devil have you been up to? Helping Rumford dig for ghosts, I see. Good God!" He was looking me up and down. I smiled with an effort.

"Your—Mr. Calder was showing me where he keeps his brandy."

"Good God, Miss Garrison!" he repeated. My knees, my body, even my hands felt suddenly weak at the sympathy and indignation in his eyes. As often happens under a sudden burst of sympathy, I felt a strong temptation to cry. I tried very hard not to. Keith gave his flashlight to his father and took me around the waist, almost boosting me along. "Your arm is badly cut. We had better get something for it. To prevent infection."

I said "Thank you," very meekly.

At the foot of the steps leading up to the tower, Freddie Calder offered us some of the brandy in the dusty bottle. "Let me open it and—"

"Freddie, do you want Miss Garrison to lose an arm?"

"No, no! What an idea, my boy! Such a lovely arm, too!" Then he saw the long, jagged mark where the rusted crucifix had dug the flesh away, and was all apologies. I was relieved when Keith sent him and Mr. Rumford back across the little courtyard to the modern half of the abbey to enjoy their brandy in warmer circles. Then he helped me up the steps, endless steps. I was deeply grateful for his help and the fact that he asked no questions. He was quiet, competent, very masculine, and although I was much too shaky and tired to appreciate his sexual appeal, I was aware of it.

"Are there a thousand steps here?" I asked finally, making an effort to joke about it. "Or only six or seven hundred?" The arm around my waist stiffened. He started to pick me up off the step. I protested that I had been joking, that I was perfectly all right, but by that time he had picked me up with an impressive ease, and I decided I had better remain still and make his job easier. He was already in the little hall outside my room. When he pushed the door open with his foot, I began to laugh.

"That's better," he said. "After that smile, you are bound to live. You looked so pale there for a few minutes, I wondered."

"It's only that you did that exactly like the movies. Kicking the door in."

Whatever his amusement, he did not show it except, perhaps, around the eyes. "It was ajar. I didn't break the lock." He set me down on the bed none too gently. He seemed to be in a hurry. I said, "I'm very grateful. You've been a terrific help. Please don't think you have to stay around wasting time on a trivial scratch."

"I don't have to stay around doing anything. Can you hold your arm out? Here. Toward the light."

I tried. It wasn't difficult. "It is nothing." As a matter of fact, I felt the whole thing was badly overrated, thanks to my stupid panic. "It is nothing."

"You repeat yourself. Let me see. Did you ever hear of septic poisoning? Of tetanus?"

I groaned. "I'm sorry you found out anything

about it. Honestly, I'll be fine after a night's sleep. I was more scared than hurt."

And then, quite suddenly, he left me. After having done my best to get rid of him, I was now crushed because he took me at my word. I was also too tired even to undress. I pulled myself higher up on the bed. The spread had been removed and a warm, woolly blanket lay under me. Nothing had ever felt so good. I was even too tired to snap off the lamp.

Only minutes later the floor creaked under a footfall. I opened my eyes. Keith Calder was back with a wide-eyed Emily and a handful of odd objects including a roll of gauze, a basin of water and some tubes of medicine, probably antibiotics, or whatever might be useful.

"For heaven's sake!" I insisted, trying to sit up. "It is only a scratch."

But together, while Emily kept making little, amazed comments heavily mingled with questions, they got my arm doctored, washed, salved, depoisoned, and finally wrapped.

"Emy, be quiet," Keith told her finally as he picked up the remnants of his surgical skills.

Emily grinned. "Keith says you were knocked in the head—or almost—by one of Leander's ghosts."

"If that is so, and I don't deny it," I admitted, stifling a yawn, "I can't prove it."

"Spooky down there, isn't it?"

Keith said calmly, "Go to bed, infant."

She shrugged, nudged me painfully so that I winced. She made a little moue of apology. "I'm glad it's you and not me they want. I've been down there. And frankly, I prefer the living."

"*Go to bed!*"

In the doorway she wrinkled her nose at her brother, waved to me, and disappeared into the darkness of the hall. Keith was smiling faintly as he turned back to me.

"How anyone that young can be ready for matrimony baffles me. I don't envy your brother. He has his work cut out for him." He looked around the room, then went to the French door and, for some reason, pushed the drape aside and peered out into the monumental darkness that was suddenly, at both borders of the vision, framed by the lights along the shore. "Somewhere over in Bristol and those other busy places, their fears are only of this world. There is something to be said for a sceptic."

"And are your fears of another world?" I asked him suddenly.

He shook his head, pulled the drape back in place and turned back to the room.

"I simply don't like what it does to perfectly normal, civilized people. In fact, I wish Leander and his manifestations would go somewhere else and practice. They won't find anything genuine here, but they may find something that—" He broke off, to my intense curiosity, and snapped off the lamp on the dressing table. He glanced at the pink lamp on the stand beside my bed. "Can you manage now?"

"Yes. Thank you."

He pointed a stern finger at me as he had done to his sister. "Go to bed!"

I laughed and he left the room, closing the door behind him with surprising care.

Sleepily, I looked at the door for a long time. I was thinking that in spite of various little mishaps, I was looking forward to my stay at Sea Abbey. Finally, after drinking the vile, chemically-flavored water in the glass by my bed, I went to sleep.

FIVE

Emily and Bob had been right when they claimed the room given to me was most comfortable and had a fabulous view. I was to discover that very shortly. Meanwhile, I was awakened by a timid knock on the door and the sound of the knob turning. Fresh from a nasty dream about tombs and dungeons, I asked anxiously,

"Who's there?"

"Maid, Miss." A pretty redhead stuck her head in. "Tea tray. I wasn't to wake you. I done it anyway. Sorry, Miss."

"No, no. It's quite all right. Just set the tray here, beside the bed. I could use that hot tea."

She did so, then went to the French door and drew the drape aside, sniffing mightily. "Real sun out there. A bit watery, but real. Have you been out on the level yet? You'll just love the view, Miss."

"The level?" I sat up, tried to stretch the muscles of my left arm but everything was stiff from my shoulder to my elbow. No matter. Otherwise, I was in good spirits, looking forward to the wedding in six days, and ready to enjoy myself.

"Ay. This little terrace. Upper level, it's called. Miss Emily's room opens onto it from the south side, but of course, she never goes out there anymore."

I looked around the bed post, through the open door. A brisk wind blew in, making me shiver. It didn't bother the redhead though. Her hair lashed around her little starched cap, flushing her healthy cheeks.

"Miss Emily doesn't go out on the terrace? Is it too cold?"

"Nothing like that, Miss. It's only that she remembers the old lady. A good soul. Had her odd ways; believed in spirits and that sort. No nonsense with her, though. Good to me. Right here it was, she went over."

I got out of bed and wrapped myself in my inadequate chiffon peignoir, slipping it first over my bandaged arm. I went to the door, stood just behind the glass, and could see now very easily how the unfortunate woman had lost her balance. Probably an attack of vertigo, and then . . . that terrible plunge to the medieval stones of the courtyard far below.

"Do come in," I said anxiously; for the girl made me nervous, leaning out over the low, crenellated wall. Teasingly, she looked back over her shoulder at me.

"Oh, but I'm that careful, Miss! Got a good balance, I have. You see how I set my foot, flat-like." She came in finally and closed the door. "It was a nasty accident, but only an accident, when all's said. And Mrs. Calder was old, you must remember."

I thought of last night and the accidental fall of the rusted crucifix. I said with a touch of irony, "There seems to be a rash of accidents at Sea Abbey."

The redhead laughed. "That's a good one, that is. And nearer true than you might think. Maybe there is something to the old lady's spooks and banshees and what-all, playing their sly tricks on a body. I wouldn't put it beyond the best of 'em. I was never one to dabble in that sort of thing. Not Dilys MacGowan. No, Miss. Not me!"

I asked with interest, "Have you been here long?"

"Since I was seventeen, Miss. That'll be six years gone by. It was hard when the Old Lady was alive, but I liked it here no matter what. She was a close one for seeing that all was done as it should be. The gentlemen, excuse me for saying, ain't so fussed up about doing things as they should be. Mister Keith, he's the one that's like the old lady, though you wouldn't think so, him being—" She looked around cautiously, "born out of wedlock, like they say. Now, you drink your tea while it's hot, Miss. It'll do you good. You're shivering."

Since she had just brought in a positive torrent of icy wind, it wasn't surprising, but I let her think what she liked, and was sorry when she went away. I realized after she had gone that despite her penchant for melodrama and an obvious enthrallment with Mr. Rumford's ghosts, she was one of the people I liked best at Sea Abbey. I had not yet seen the housekeeper, Mrs. Milligan, and the man who served us at dinner last night had been so old I feared for his every creaking move, poor man! Clearly, he was an old retainer.

And then, absurdly enough, as soon as I had drunk the strong dark, peat-tasting tea, I bathed and dressed and went out on "the upper level" myself to find out what was so dangerous about it. I soon discovered. The wind was strong, as I had expected. Almost overpowering, I found, the minute I took the third step and reached the crenellations that were less than three feet high. It seemed to me that when the wind swept wildly around the corners from either direction, it was nearly strong enough to push a person off the little terrace, over that entirely inadequate wall. However, the situation had obviously existed for centuries, and since I myself would not be using the upper level for very long, it was hardly my concern.

Still, I thought, as I stepped backward, closer to the aged gray stone of the tower, it might be possible to get Bob to have that low wall raised, once he was married and had the right to make suggestions. Bob was very wise for his age, and while his settlement, when he reached twenty-one, would be considerable, I knew I could trust him if I raised that settlement. In years to come, when he was twenty-five, for instance, he would receive another two million dollars, and by the time he was thirty, he would be handling his entire fortune, probably mine, too: for as the years went by, I had more and more confidence in him.

"Easy, Nell! Take care!" cried a male voice carried on the cold, morning wind.

I whirled around but did not make the mistake of stepping out to find this disembodied voice. I knew it was Duncan Calder, and I was annoyed to have someone watching me. I looked below, far below, until I saw the man in khaki shorts and shirt like his brother, all legs and partially bared chest. He was waving to me from the courtyard. Very carefully, I made my way—only two short steps—to the crenellated wall where I looked over and waved to him.

"Hey, there! Watch it, girl!" That was Duncan again, imitating something he probably thought was an American gangster.

He amused me, but did not incite me to do anything dangerous, like lean over the little wall.

"Coming to breakfast? Or will you have it in your room? Do come along. It's damnably dull without you. And no pleasure for me at all."

I only hoped Bessie was not an audience to all this meaningless byplay. I had no wish to act as a wedge between Bessie and Duncan. There was a lot about poor Bessie that appealed to me. We had a great deal in common. I waved and moved back into my room and closed the French door. After checking and tucking in the windblown strands of my hair, I went down the long series of stone steps to the main floor passage. I looked furtively into the darkness that led to the damp stone interior of the ancient abbey church, and with a shudder, turned my back on it and started across the courtyard.

I felt a little awkward to see that Duncan had waited for me. His untidy, bronze-colored hair blew in the wind and his big grin, framed by his short beard, made me think, for some curious reason, of his young sister.

"Good Lord, Nell! What happened to you? Fall out of bed?"

I laughed, though I did not find this remark precisely sidesplitting. "One of Mr. Rumford's ghosts was playing tricks in that abbey vault of yours."

"Oh-oh. Sounds as though Dad went searching for the old brandy bottle. That's his favorite ploy with beautiful women." He took my arm and in spite of my feeling that his grin was too easy, his friendship a little too generous, I could not resist the young giant's gravitational pull.

"I take it he often searches for the brandy bottle."

He looked at me innocently. "No. Only when there's a rich—that is—a beautiful visitor."

"Preferably beautiful *and* rich."

He stopped as we entered the modern half of the abbey. I did not glance at him. I found my fingernails intensely interesting. He chuckled, deep in his throat. A very masculine, deeply bronzed throat like his brother's. I suspected very little really troubled him, even my straight-to-the-target remark.

"You know Father remarkably well in such a short time. Or have you met him before? I mean to say—did someone tell you . . . what kind of person he was?"

I did not answer immediately. I was trying to think of how I could answer without giving away my private opinion of Freddie Calder. After all, I was, in a sense, about to become a member of the family, and I preferred it to be on a friendly basis.

"I think he must have a fondness for brandy," I said at last, looking as innocent as he.

"That's Father," he agreed, clearly relieved. "A bit of a nip before bedtime. He—" He paused just long enough to lick his heavy, sensuous lips. "He means well, actually. And—" he added eagerly, "he is exceedingly fond of you. Anyone can see that."

"Thank you," I said, hardly knowing what else I could say that would not betray my real feelings.

I was actually relieved when I made out his wife's yellow-white head in the obscurity of the hall before us.

"I might have known you'd be shillyshallying around this awful place, Dunc. Anything to avoid me."

I wasn't sure whether she had seen me until I spoke, "Good morning, Mrs. Calder," and saw to it that there was considerable space between her husband and myself. I hoped my observation of her was genuine, that she seemed, oddly enough, to like me.

"Oh, it's you, Elinor. Good morning. Lord! What's happened? You fell down those stupid stairs! I almost did, once. I can't stand that half of the building. When are they going to tear it down like anybody sensible would do?"

Duncan tagged along behind us as we went in to breakfast together. I didn't bother to explain about my accident. It was unpleasant even to think of now. Except for the kindness of Keith and Emily, last evening still lingered with me as a horror. And then I thought of Keith and wondered if he would be at breakfast.

He was not. All the rest of the family were there, and so was Leander Rumford, busy eating cutlets and eggs and some sort of stiff-looking fish. Kippers, I suppose. He looked up as if delighted when he saw me. The others, Freddie Calder, Emily and Bob, were friendly and inquired about my night, whether I had slept well.

While Bob was in the midst of asking about my arm, little Leander said enthusiastically, "Have you thought about your rare talent with the Other World, Miss Garrison? You must be very proud of your accomplishments in drawing them out."

Bob, however, was in a touchy mood. I was secretly proud of him. He might so easily have let the Calders babble on about my amusing, if unfortunate, adventure, and simply said nothing.

"What the devil do you mean, Rumford, by saying Nell should be proud she almost got killed in that damned tomb? You don't get me into that place. How the devil did you get my sister down there?"

Everyone got very upset and started to make excuses. Even I joined the apologists. Then I broke it off nervously, laughing, waving my good hand and dismissing the matter. I knew I had to do something. Emily was already looking angrily at Bob and obviously ready to explode.

"Please!" I told them as Freddie and Duncan pulled my chair out for me. "This is all very silly. My arm is much better this morning. Emily and Keith helped me enormously last night, wrapping the little scratch, cleaning it. Thank you, Emily. You were a great help."

The girl subsided, smiling at me across the table a little shyly. Presently, during breakfast, I saw her slip her thin, brown hand along the tablecloth to Bob who squeezed her fingers in relief.

Both Freddie Calder and Duncan suggested presently that they show me around the island after breakfast. This led to a mild argument between them that each had work to do and therefore the other couldn't possibly show anyone around the island.

"But I thought there wasn't any island. Just the abbey on solid rock," I objected in surprise before I realized I was insulting everyone at the long table. Even Bob became indignant.

"Nell! This happens to be a very famous island. I don't think you realize just how important it is. Certainly, there's nothing else except St. Michael's Mount off Penzance to equal it. Why don't you let someone show it to you as they want to? You'll be impressed. I wish I could go with you, but I've got to go ashore and check with the vicar who will be here to marry us." He looked warmly at Emily who grinned back, her eyes sparkling with delight. "We thought we'd have him here overnight and make it festive."

I was almost as enthused as Emily. "That should be wonderful. Where will the ceremony take place?"

Mr. Rumford suggested brightly, "To be quite proper, it should take place before the altar—" He nodded to me. "The altar with the crucifix restored to its natural place in the old abbey vault. You remember the exact spot, Miss Garrison."

We all stared at him. Emily tittered and covered her mouth. Freddie started to laugh but cut off the sound. I am not sure that Bessie understood the black humor of the suggestion after last night's episode, and while Duncan and Bob looked as though they would protest, Bob with anger, Bessie scoffed,

"Don't be ridiculous. We'd all die of pneumonia in that hole. It ought to be in a nice, cozy place like— well—" She shrugged. "You see what I mean."

I was beginning to see that if we all listened to Bessie she would bring us back to earth, sane and sensible earth.

When breakfast was over Freddie and Emily introduced me to stout, strong-jawed little Mrs. Milligan, the housekeeper, who looked me over sternly and then shook her head. For a few seconds I stood there in the long dining hall feeling exactly like a girl being interviewed for her first job.

"You're a fool, Madam. I'll say that to your face."

While Freddie started a nervous protest, I noted with curiosity that Emily was amused.

"How—what have I done to make you think that, Mrs. Milligan?"

"Ye've let them put you in old Mrs. Calder's room. A strong lady was Mrs. Calder. But she found it was unlucky up there. And so it was."

I was fumbling for a polite excuse though it was hardly my fault, when I saw the Irish twinkle of humor in Mrs. Milligan's eyes.

"No matter. We'll look out for you. That we will, Miss Elinor."

"Thank you, Mrs. Milligan. I'll count on you for precisely that."

After this, I felt considerably more at home among the Calders, or at any rate, those who were left on the island after Emily insisted on going with Bob because her health was perfect and there was no likelihood of any more stomach trouble. "It was something I ate, I tell you."

Which may have been true, but did not remove the danger.

Mr. Rumford went off to test for psychic manifestations. "I must work on various spots before Mr. Keith sends me about my business. He has a way of vanquishing any manifestations that might otherwise come to me."

Freddie explained, upon being prodded by Duncan, that he had to write another note. "On business, of course. I thought we might make this one of the Stately Homes of England."

With a great deal of manufactured enthusiasm I agreed that this was a fine idea, but knowing Freddie now, I wasn't surprised to find there was a catch to it.

"I shall naturally require something above one hundred thousand pounds to make the abbey safe for all the Yankee tourists. The clumsy clods are sure to fall into holes, and lose their little toddlers in the vaults and otherwise require a perfection only satisfied by money." He peered at me and repeated with care, "Only satisfied by money."

"How true!" I agreed and was relieved when, at that moment, Bessie broke in rudely,

"You coming, Nell? I'll give you the Stately Homes Tour of Sea Abbey and it won't cost you a shilling— Pardon! Ten pence."

Duncan said, "Shall I trot along with you ladies?"

To my surprise, his wife said, "No. Run along and help your brother dig up old bones."

"Goblets and chalices and crucifixes, Bessie-girl. Not bones."

But she shrugged off these details and I found myself following her out to the courtyard where I discovered there was an unobtrusive little door in the corner of the "modern" section of the abbey. From there there was a narrow walk open to the windswept sky and to the channel waters far below on our left. I stayed close to the abbey wall, wondering all the time why in a thousand years someone hadn't thought to fence or wall up this picturesque little walk.

"Where does it lead to?" I asked Bessie, who was holding her hair as if she expected it to fly off.

"Duncan explained it to me once. If you think of the island as a ship and the modern half here as the forward part, then we're walking toward the prow. Makes a bit of sense, actually."

Anything might make sense except the fact that this

tricky little walk had no safety rail. It was a potential disaster of the kind terribly common at Sea Abbey. From this walk we could see Bob and Emily starting off for the shore and the little town of Abbeyvue. They seemed very happy. At least, Emily was gay and laughing. Bob, at the motor, looked very much the master of the household. He shook his head and made some sort of remark. She clapped her hands, laughing again. Knowing Bob, I was sure he told her he was about to buy the Calders a new boat. And then I remembered the little distinction between Duncan and Keith. Duncan had thought it was a great idea. Keith had said angrily that all they needed was a new motor. I hoped my prejudice did not show. God knows, I was delighted to be able to buy boats for people, but it was very pleasant to have a proud acquaintance like Keith refuse it. Yet Duncan was right. Bob could afford it. It was nonsense that they should have to get along as they did with that feeble old boat.

"Come along. Don't dawdle," Bessie called. She was surprisingly agile herself and I was much ashamed not to be able to keep up with her. I started walking, hurried my steps, found myself very close to tumbling over in a hail of broken rock and shale, and decided not to be quite so quick to answer a Calder challenge. The waters licking the rugged rock walls of the island did not look friendly.

By gingerly keeping to the center of the little path, I managed to reach the "prow" of the island. The Calders were right. There actually was an island here underfoot. At any rate, I saw a small patch of earth, triangular in shape, running down over the face of a cliff. At the bottom there was a patch of earth and stones close to the water, so that the foam rolled over an area about four yards long, and hardly more than a yard wide.

"This is the island part of Sea Abbey," Bessie told me as I stared. She laughed at my surprise.

"This is all of the earth on the island?"

"All that's left. The abbey is built over some earth, of course. But it's a grim place altogether. Believe me, it takes a good, stiff bit of the Old Guinness, or better yet, that peaty Irish whiskey to keep me here." She looked at me, her pale eyes saying a good deal more. "And that's what I wanted to talk to you about."

"You wanted to talk to me? I don't understand. Is something wrong?"

"Only if you let it be." She waited for that to soak in. I wondered if she was afraid I might make a play for her husband and I wished I could reassure her without insulting that nice, friendly fellow who was the last man in the world I would dream of making a deliberate play for.

I cleared my throat, looked around, and bundled myself against the fierce wind. "I really would rely upon your opinion, or your advice. I think you know that."

"Good. Because you're going to need it. They're a nasty lot, these Calders. I'm not making any claims about the bastard—" I started, but of course, she was quite right. Keith was a bastard in the legal sense. "Sure. He's a good one, maybe. Too moody and serious for old Bessie. But I'd trust him. On the other hand, I think you ought to know that before you came, there was all kinds of talk about your money. Even from your brother. I mean—he wasn't against the idea at all."

Bewildered, I asked, "What idea? That I would leave my money to him in my will? Bob knows that. It's no secret, surely."

"No. A little more direct. They'd like to have all your money themselves, I think."

A chill caught at me that had nothing to do with the brisk wind. "You aren't talking about murder!"

"Gawd, no! That's the hard way. There's a much easier way. To marry you and get your damned dollars that way."

"Freddie, of course."

She nodded. "Freddie first. But if that don't work, if you ask me, they'll force Keith onto you. He may not want to do anything so rotten"—I looked at her. She didn't even blink—"as to marry you for your money, I mean. But he may do it for the family. He figures he owes them a lot. They took him in. Made him welcome. They didn't have to, you know. They've really been quite fair to him. So—to pay them back, he might just make love to you, put you on, as they say, to help the family."

I had never been so boldly and frankly told my own worthlessness. Not only that, but worse. It killed in me, or nearly killed, that first liking, the interest I felt in Keith Calder, because I thought he was the one person here at Sea Abbey who might be perfectly sincere with me. The one other, if you counted the blunt and direct Bessie Calder.

I hesitated. The wind swept across our faces and I put my hand up to protect my hair. At the same time Bessie fell against me and then swung around with her hands over her ears and backed up.

"Oh, Christ! Inside, or I'll lose my scalp."

A little like a genie in a bottle, Bessie vanished from my side. She backed up the path behind us and at the top, which looked equal to the second floor of the modern abbey, she pushed against a heavy iron-bound door. Somewhat to my surprise, the door opened in a most obliging way and since I didn't want to be out on this narrow ledge path alone, I hurried up after her. At the door I stopped a minute, looked back at the view of the ruffled waters ahead, and then at the busy landscapes on both sides. I was trying to get my bearings so that I could face everyone without that abused and pitiful look I secretly felt I must present to those who knew I liked Keith Calder already.

Going inside, I half expected to find myself in one of those ill-lighted, rock-walled passages that honeycombed this infernal abbey. The hall was hardly Buckingham Palace, but the stone walls were whitewashed, the low, beamed ceiling of the hall was likewise painted white. Though there was no window or other method of illumination except the electric line running boldly along the wall, there was a dim light provided from some mysterious source, along with a sound of irregular knocking.

But Bessie was nowhere in sight.

Remembering the idiotic events of a pseudo-psychic nature that had occurred since my arrival yesterday afternoon, I lost all patience, not only with the abbey but with myself for being so easily unnerved by these asinine happenings. I called to Bessie, realized she had gone around the ell in the hall, and started after her. The light ahead was a little more illuminating, but I could not see Bessie.

On the right of the hall were narrow doors much like those downstairs that had, I supposed, once been the monkish sleeping cells. I tried the first door. It was a hideous little place, truly a cell, with a tiny, high window filled with stained glass that even I recognized as rather amateurish work. It also kept the room unconscionably dark. The place had the moist, gloomy look of a stone tomb that marked most of this medieval structure.

Worse, however, Bessie lay crumpled up on the floor in a faint. The floor was thinly carpeted, and a flamboyant large compact, opened with the mirror prominently displayed, rolled off by itself. Bessie's

wig was perched over one ear. Obviously, she had
been arranging her wig by the dark view from her
compact. And something had stopped her. Something
that made her crumple up in a dead faint.

SIX

It was so dark in the little cell that I could hardly see to rouse Bessie, but at least her heart was beating, and she didn't appear to have any physical injuries. I got up, went back to the door into the hall and pushed it open wide, hoping to borrow more light from that dim glow around the corner of the hall ahead.

When I returned to Bessie, she moved faintly. I called to her. "Bessie! Mrs. Calder!" I raised my voice, shook her a little, but gently. I could not be sure some internal trouble hadn't brought on the faint.

Hearing a persistent tapping somewhere, I got up, went back into the hall and hurried a few steps further around the sharply turning hall. I nearly ran into a flight of stone steps. Still in sight several steps down toward the main floor was Keith Calder, surrounded by blocks of stone, a lot of chipped dust and pebbles, an electric light overhead and a hole in the wall before him that was so eery I almost recoiled. I called to him. He looked up, clearly astonished to see me or anyone else.

"Come quickly! It's Mrs. Calder. She fainted."

He set the chisel down beside a knife and several curiously ordinary kitchen instruments. I had more than half expected such interests as his required instruments similar to those in a surgical operation, or at the very least, a dentist's office. Keith strode past me as I pointed the way. By the time we reached Bessie he was running. He knelt beside her and cradled her against his body.

"What the devil? She doesn't seem to have slipped or fallen . . . Bessie?" His voice was suddenly and surprisingly gentle.

By this time, to my enormous relief, Bessie was beginning to come around, feebly clawing the air. Gradually, her eyelids flickered and she looked up at Keith.

"Oh! It's you. Gawd! Ye're good to see. I thought you might be that thing . . . That floating—" She sat up, clutched her head dizzily. "You see anything?"

Keith and I exchanged puzzled glances. Bessie looked around and then pointed at the doorway with an arm that trembled. We both stared but couldn't figure out what she saw. Keith asked, "Was it someone who frightened you?"

"It—it was what I saw. I thought it was in the doorway. One of your—creatures."

I murmured, "Those stories about the bodies in the walls."

"Bess," Keith murmured, "you know that psychic chap is conjuring up fairy tales. You know perfectly well there are no ghosts."

"But it was right in the doorway, I think. I was doing my hair and I saw this shadow in the mirror of my compact. And what with this creepy mausoleum, and my nerves so damned jumpy ever since that Rumford fellow got on this island, well, I got scared clear to the bone." She looked up at me.

I said, "It is all exactly the way I feel when I wander through here. I can imagine—or even see—all sorts of things. Or someone may be in here trying to frighten us."

Keith looked at me sharply. "Who would be doing that? And why?"

"Not to drive you off, Nell. Not until a few things have taken place, anyway," Bessie put in with one of those too-obvious looks that Keith must have read very easily. I tried to pretend I did not understand her. But at all events, Keith was good to his sister-in-law, and coaxed her quietly,

"We know what you mean, Bess, and how you feel. It is because you don't understand our work, Duncan's and mine. But you must not be afraid of it. Or of us. And whatever it was that you saw, it is gone now. Are you able to walk? We'll get you out of here. This place is too damp and depressing at best."

But Bessie suddenly grabbed her head and then pushed Keith away.

"I am perfectly splendid. You run along. I'll—I'll join you."

I had a notion that she wanted to adjust that magnificent blonde wig of hers and preferred to do it without a man watching her. I caught Keith's eye. Somehow, he understood and, having helped Bessie to her feet, he went to the doorway, looking around as if he half expected to see the curious shadow that had frightened her.

I was beginning to believe that, like me, she had let her imagination get the better of her. It was easy enough, at Sea Abbey, to imagine all sorts of ghostly visitations.

To keep his attention directed away from Bessie while she made herself glamorous again, I asked Keith, half-joking, "Were you telling us the truth when you said you never see ghosts in this place? I imagine you must have been digging for your precious bodies back in that hideous hole on the staircase."

He smiled, shook his head. "Actually, the body problem is a hindrance. Any artifacts we may discover and turn over to the museums are totally unconnected with the walling up of the convicts back in the late eighteenth century. Our discoveries date over seven hundred years before that savage, Duncan Calder."

"Savage . . . What on earth do you mean?"

Belatedly, he realized that I was unaware of one bit of information that was rather important in this connection.

"That amiable ancestor who contracted to ship convicts to Australia and landed them instead at Sea Abbey was also named Duncan Calder. It is the name of the eldest—" He paused, his lips twisting just a trifle. "The eldest legitimate son of the Calder house." He assured me with just a trace of irony, "There are no other similarities, I assure you. My brother lacks our ancestor's bloodthirsty practicality."

"I didn't think so. That is—I never meant—nothing."

He looked at me for a moment I found uncomfortably long. What was he thinking? Was he scheming how to marry me if his father failed in the family attempt to gain my money? Or was I simply misled by Bessie's warning which may, or may not, have been genuine? Was there some personal jealousy involved? Not that Bessie had any personal interest in Keith Calder, but she might be anxious for me to leave Sea Abbey before I became attached to her flirtatious husband. There might be many reasons why Bessie had warned me, not all of them helpful to me.

It was unfortunate that Keith attracted me so much. I must remember at all times to be on my guard against that attraction, because there was every good chance that Bessie knew what she was talking about in warning me. The Calders had probably guessed after last night that I was never going to warm up to Freddie Calder. And who else was handy and available? Keith!

Keith said suddenly, "You aren't enjoying it much here, are you?"

I looked my most innocent, which may not have been as successful as I hoped.

"Of course, I am. Though, naturally, I was upset about Mrs. Calder's faint."

"And last night? How do you explain that painful business with your arm? Emily and I were rather . . . concerned. It seemed an extraordinarily inhospitable thing to have happen to our guest."

I wiggled my fingers and pinched my lower arm, saying gaily, "Nothing to it, thanks to you and Emily. You both were an enormous help. It was a lucky accident, your finding us in that—tomb. And I am glad Emily has her room on the same level as mine. Just in case."

"It was no accident that I came upon you in that tomb."

As I watched him, startled, he reached over and pinched my stiffly bandaged upper arm. I winced and he contradicted me almost angrily. "You see. The pain is not gone. There was a great deal more to it than you will admit. Thank you for that. You are being very good about the whole affair."

I shrugged. "I hardly notice it unless people go around pinching me. Anyway, it was only an accident." When I mentioned his pinching me, he winced as if personally attacked, but I gave him a big smile, and was conscious of the thaw in our relations.

I was acutely aware of how close we were in that little, half-dark hall and from the way his gaze shifted to my mouth, I had a pulsating, delightful sensation that he was thinking about kissing me. I could not think, offhand, of a single reason why I opposed the idea, and was even temptingly ready for this pleasant assault.

But that ended with Bessie's flat, eminently practical voice. "Righto. I'm near as good as new. You ready to move on, Nell?"

I wasn't, but concealing a sigh, I said I was. Keith moved away, ahead of us.

"I'll clear the inside steps. They bring you out near the lounge on the ground floor. There are endless passages in this labyrinth, but if you know the combination, it isn't too difficult." He looked back at me. "Providing you don't go wandering about the ancient sector, where there are so many holes, so many deep drops, left by the Calder Moles of the past, that you aren't likely to find them to your liking in any case."

When she supposed he could not hear us, Bessie whispered wisely. "Remember what I told you about him. And the others. The Calder charm, and all."

I was dying to remind her snappishly, "I can take care of myself!" but I bit off that discourteous reply and simply looked ahead as if I had neither heard nor understood her.

It was less easy to pass Keith's place of work without looking at that weird hole, or at least giving it a lingering glance. Both Bessie and I stopped on the step landing. Keith looked back at us, his hands full of the instruments he had picked up from the step.

"Coming?"

Bessie said, "Righto, Keith. Quite a hole you've got there. You trying to get my leg broken or something? Find any treasures?"

Meanwhile, I was staring into the hole at which Keith had been working. It was, unfortunately for my imagination, nothing but a hole, revealing a lot of crumbled gray stuff, probably mortar, a little dirt, and a great deal of broken stone.

"Find anything exciting?" Keith asked, catching me redhanded, so to speak.

I looked around, pretending an absolute indifference to his scorn, but he was smiling. Bessie pulled at my sleeve.

"You haven't seen the rooms downstairs, and the places where my Duncan works."

I wanted to say, "Never mind; forget the tour," because I had no desire to find myself in something like last night's hellhole, but as I had no excuse, I went meekly along after breaking down and returning Keith's smile.

Afterward, I tried to find out from Bessie just what Keith was doing and if all the work done by him and by his brother was equally baffling. Somewhat to my surprise, Bessie hadn't the smallest idea of what her husband accomplished, or what the technical problems were.

"It's just a hole. That's all. Always a hole. Nothing to see. Sort of like digging out a body in a graveyard, bit by bit, and then stuffing it into another grave in a museum."

"Ugh!"

"Oh, well, lads will be lads, they keep telling me when I ask questions of anyone else." She shrugged. "They find their bit of trash for the museums or wherever. But nothing to interest me, I can tell you. A little jewel now and then? A ring, maybe. Anything worth looking at, worth wearing. But no. It's all for museums and that mish-mash."

I found I had to give up as a futile job this attempt to find out what was going on in Keith's and Duncan's work, and after the nervewracking affair of Bessie's unexpected collapse, I too was badly shaken. I would like to have gone walking by myself and perhaps watch for the return of Emily and Bob across the choppy sunlit channel, but Bessie had me in tow and didn't want to give up her job as a talkative and not entirely trustworthy guide. I asked her how she felt, if her head ached, if she had hurt herself in her fall, but she insisted that she was perfectly all right and the air would "do both of us good."

So she showed me over the long northern side of the island, especially the huge, badly rusted portcullis which looked as though it had rusted into its place at the top of a series of steps above an iron door. This, Bessie assured me, hadn't been opened in the memory of anyone living.

"The current's rough. Nobody enters by this side of the island. I suppose, the way these Calders used to live, they needed two exits."

I laughed. "And those horrible teeth up there were for chewing out the enemy? Or were they used to trap the police?"

We both studied the portcullis overhead. The truth is, I hadn't been entirely joking. Those ugly, rusted teeth did look capable of chewing up—if not a regiment—at least a full company.

"We best go inside," Bessie said, clutching her head. "Duncan hates me all blowsy."

"Where is he, by the way?"

She crooked her forefinger, and when I approached at this signal, she said, "Look through this hole between the blocks of the wall. Here."

I followed her advice, peered through and saw nothing but rocks and the channel below. I said, "I don't see him. Is he down there?"

"No, you silly clot! He's opposite you. Working on the outside of the wall. Listen now for the hammer and chisel."

We listened. Nothing. I did hear the waves hit the rocks far below. That was all. Bessie applied her own eye to the hole in the wall. I, personally, felt like Pyramis and Thisbe, foolishly escaped from *Midsummer Night's Dream*.

"Well, I'm damned!"

"Maybe he's taking five," I suggested, not caring too much.

"Five what? He told me he'd be finishing yesterday's barrow."

"Barrow!"

She shrugged. "That's a joke. These diggers, the real ones, I mean, they have barrows and all sorts of crazy activities, just like moles. I think, usually, the barrows run like—well—like graves, or like the way the rocks run. But it's all like moles. I put a little money into Duncan's work when I first married him, but now—forget it! I'm not about to run dry on account of him and his moles. He and Keith, they make jokes. They pretend they are real archaeologists discovering Stonehenge or something. They're . . . well, Dunc is a fake. I don't know why Keith encourages him. He just plays at it."

She stalked off across the courtyard. "Now, I've got to comb this hellish place to find Dunc."

"Why, for heaven's sake?"

"Why? Because . . . never mind. You're not a wife. You wouldn't know." With this cryptic remark, she left me to my own devices which, though unexpected, suited me very well.

Wondering with some amusement where Duncan Calder was, I had a fairly good idea that he would be unlikely to be found working. I had never been sure how he made his living; perhaps like his father, as the Squire of Sea Abbey. Mrs. Milligan came by, rolling a big, sealed can which proved to be garbage. I don't know where I thought they stored and destroyed it, but as it turned out, she was bringing it to the steps above the landing where a boat of the Abbeyvue Sanitary organization would take it ashore. Life on an island, even this close to shore, was hardly an idyll.

I went over to the ancient half of the abbey, looked down that ominous passage which led to Freddie's liquor and the unsteady crucifix, and then I turned and went up the steps. I was curious about the other parts of the tower, those below mine, and stopped at the first level. Bob's room was along here somewhere. I passed two doors. There was a third door that opened onto a tiny terrace similar to the one outside my own room. I stepped outside.

The wind had died down and as in most so-called civilized areas, smog began to roll in, coiling around the abbey with quick, serpent wiggles like a Sidewinder. It was easy to see that a big city like Bristol was not too far—or not far enough—away. I tried to make out the boat Bob and Emily had taken. There was a small craft halfway to the Abbeyvue harbor but I couldn't tell, in this heavy air, whether it was coming or going. I started back into the tower. I was stopped by voices somewhere not far away. I couldn't make them out at first. They were talking in the doorway of a room. Mine, probably. It was overhead and a little to the right of me that I placed the sounds.

A young woman giggled. "Master Duncan, you are the one! You'd charm the birds out of the trees, you would! But you'll not be making fast and loose of little Dilys, let me tell you." Her voice was stifled. He had undoubtedly pulled her back into the room and was kissing her. Bessie knew her husband very well. That much was plain to me.

Curious, I watched from below. In a minute, pert, pretty Dilys, looking slightly tousled, reached out, shook a pillowcase, and stepped back into my room, closing the French door. I waited, hoping she or Duncan would leave so I could come into my room without witnessing what might eventually be a messy domestic crisis.

Voices were audible again, this time going down the stairs toward this level. Duncan was saying, "Dilys, my girl, you're way out when you think I'm not worth it. I'll be solid as the Bank of England in a little while. Only a little. Give me that."

"I'm givin' you the back of my hand, Mister Duncan. I don't hold with such goings-on. I'm an honest girl, I am."

"The trouble with you, Dilys, is you've no imagination. And no faith in me. You'll find it pays dividends."

"Oh, bosh! What an idiot you take me for!"

They went on down arguing, although it seemed fairly obvious that if they weren't lovers, they were at least moving in that direction. Apparently, Dilys was a girl who looked out for herself, and for her bank balance. I waited until they were gone from my sight and then I took the steps up to my room.

It was, of course, no surprise to me to find that the room looked different, the bed made, the makeup table dusted, my toilet articles scooted to one side for the purpose. Obviously, Dilys had been in my room for a perfectly legitimate reason. Duncan had merely followed her up here to tease and fondle her, and to indicate as was now clear to me, that if she stuck by him, or perhaps merely accepted his attentions, he would make it worth her while.

With his wife's money? Or mine?

And how did he intend to get control of Bessie's fortune and estate? Already, as I remembered from their argument about his visit to Bath, Bessie was aware of nearly every check he cashed, every shilling of hers that he used. She wasn't going to be easy to fool if he started making large, generous offers to Dilys. As long as Bessie lived, I thought, she would hold onto her money, the one sure string she had on her husband.

As long as she lived. . . .

SEVEN

I was conscious of a great coldness and went and examined my door opening onto the upper level. It was not quite latched. I worked on it. The door was slightly swollen or warped. I closed it carefully, then stood there studying my room. Suddenly, on impulse, I went over to the wardrobe and opened it. At first glance, all seemed well and as it should be. But as I examined each garment I saw that a dinner dress and a coat were hung up backwards, something that I never did.

"Dilys," I thought, "were you dressing to bring out those money promises from Duncan Calder?"

Actually, it occurred to me as I rehung the items, it need not have been Dilys who took down and then returned the clothes. Almost anyone else might have done so, except Bessie who had been with me all morning. There were several female servants, some I hadn't even seen yet. This naturally led to further suspicions. I looked over my clothes again, trying to remember exactly what I had brought with me from Paris.

There was something missing. It was my gold knit Dior suit. Was it stolen? Possibly. It might seem to someone at Sea Abbey that I had so many clothes I wouldn't remember one outfit, more or less. I didn't know whether to play detective and try to find the culprit as well as the suit, or simply to laugh and assume my suit would be returned when it had served the wearer's purpose. I suppose I was hoping against hope that Emily Calder was not the guilty party.

But Emily had expressed special interest in my clothes, hadn't she? And she might consider the whole thing a joke.

I decided to bide my time, hoping for the best. I did not want the Calders and their servants to think I had an inordinate fondness for expensive wardrobes. Though perhaps I did!

There was a growing accumulation of reasons why I should leave Sea Abbey, perhaps even before the wedding. Too much was happening that verged on serious unpleasantness.

I began to cough. The air had gradually become thick and yellowish with smoke and fog. I went over to the door, looked out. The sun was hidden behind the afternoon haze. Far below me in the courtyard Keith Calder was headed toward the south door which opened out upon the landing and flight of worn stone steps to the arriving boat below. He heard me cough and looked up, shaded his eyes, and saw me. He waved and went on. Like a schoolgirl with a crush, I found myself arguing "I really shouldn't leave here until after the wedding. Bob would never forgive me. And there are other reasons . . . one other reason . . ."

Emily and Bob and a lean, dark, youngish man were climbing the steps. The lean man had an Abe Lincoln face and wore a reversed collar. So he was the vicar Bob was going to consult. I hadn't expected him to arrive so soon, but was delighted to see him. The presence of a man of God here at Sea Abbey made me feel a good deal better. Surely, no one would go on playing tricks under his very eyes!

I watched Bob, the vicar and Emily enter the court-yard. The wind was down but the air was still filthy and active. It blew aside the skirt of Emily's mackinaw. I stared. There was the narrow, gold knit skirt of my Dior suit, revealed briefly before she hurried to close her raincoat. Then she looked toward the upper level of the tower. Her brother Keith said something, smiling, but she did not immediately share his friendly mood.

I called, "Good afternoon, everybody. Rough trip?"

I didn't know yet what my attitude about the "borrowed suit" was going to be. It was one of those times when I didn't like either alternative. I wished very much that I had never known about it. Then she might replace the suit and nobody, including me, would be the wiser.

Meanwhile, and very belatedly, young Emily waved to me, smiling that winning, seventeen-year-old smile. I waved back. It wasn't too late yet. Perhaps she intended to return the outfit and play it as a childish prank. I devoutly hoped so.

When I went down to a late lunch, however, Emily was back in her beat-up, plaid mini-skirt, playfully joking about calling off the wedding and thus confounding not only Bob, "but more important, all the businesses involved. Like yours, Reverend Hawkins, and Mrs. Milligan's—she's to do the wedding cake. And—and—Dowlinger's Smart Shoppe in Abbeyvue for my wedding gown . . . I picked it out today, Nell. Oh! It's really the end! A stunner. All beige. And mini-length."

"Beige!" I repeated in surprise.

"Mini-length!" Bessie echoed, even more aghast.

The men all laughed, but I think they found Emily's modern ideas more horrifying than we did.

I expected any minute to have Emily bring up the matter of the gold suit, but nothing was said. I felt awkward, secretive, as if it were all my fault. It was I who had done something vaguely dishonest and kept it a secret . . . I had known about the suit but said nothing. Like a spider waiting for the right time to enmesh the poor girl. In view of this sudden guilt complex, I made up my mind not to say anything about it at all. But there I was, all the same, thinking about it!

Keith asked how Bessie was. "I hope there were no bad effects." I don't know if he did it deliberately, to rouse Duncan to some sort of conjugal concern, but it worked.

"What's this, Bess old girl?" he demanded, giving his wife one of his big, contagious grins as he took her hand over the grayish-colored tapioca pudding. "Now, what have you been up to while I was—as the Yanks call it so expressively—bringing home the bacon?"

This struck me as pretty nervy of him, considering what I knew, but he had apparently reached the happy state of believing his own words. He looked perfectly open and above-board about it.

Bessie flushed a little. She had a very good complexion, one of those moist English ones where the blush was even, not mottled, and she looked genuinely pretty at her husband's interest.

"Me? Oh, I dunno. I'd say it was as near nothing as makes no matter."

"Nothing!" I exclaimed. "You fainted and might have been hurt."

There was an odd little pause, some kind of silence at the table that seemed to unite all the Calders except Keith together in a common bond of tension. There was something here they didn't like. Only in Keith's eyes I saw genuine concern for the possibility of Bessie's serious accident. I studied Emily only briefly. She had an inquisitive teen-ager's look, more interest than concern, which was not surprising. From what I

had heard of Bessie's almost public complaints about
the money-hungry Calders, I saw no reason for any
attachment on Emily's part. Freddie was rather like
his daughter, interested, even slightly sympathetic,
perhaps. It was Duncan whose reaction I studied.
Duncan was the man who had promised Dilys so
many things. Did he expect to get them from his
wife? From his wife's estate? Was it conceivable that
he and the other Calders wanted Bessie dead?

It was hard to read anything in Duncan's big, almost hyper-masculine face behind that contagious,
friendly look. He was so likable! But many a likable
face might conceal . . . What? I didn't honestly believe he would kill his wife, or anyone else, unless
driven to it by uncharacteristic anger.

Chubby little Leander Rumford, the psychic researcher, was present at the meal, and after the awkward behavior of the Calders over Bessie's accident,
Mr. Rumford's ramblings were more than welcome,
not only to me but, I thought, to Keith as well. It was
amusing to see Mr. Rumford trying to bring a smile
to the cadaverous-looking face of the young vicar.

"Almost like one of those odd-looking contraptions
people in the States use to find water. Leads me
directly to any place where there may be an other-
worldly light. What do you call those curious
branches?" He looked at me.

"Dowsing rods?" I suggested uncertainly.

This delighted the little researcher who leaped onto
it and pursued it and teased it around like a puppy on
an old sock. But I regret to say the cadaverous young
man merely looked blank. He understood neither the
excited ramblings of Mr. Rumford nor my fumbling
attempt to clear up the mystery. When Mr. Rumford
paused for breath and the Calders continued to eat, almost furtively, my brother Bob spoke up, apparently

feeling, as I did, that the situation was somewhat strained.

"You use a dowsing rod to find your ghosts, Leander?"

"Not precisely. That about the dowsing branch was a mere—a simple turn of phrase. But my efforts to reach the spirits in these fabulous walls are much like invisible sticks . . . rods . . . reaching out to these poor creatures who want to be released."

Without consciously seeking, I met Keith's eyes. To my surprise, he looked so disgusted he seemed almost angry.

"Fools!" he mouthed, his eyes rolling skyward expressively. I tried not to smile. Keith did not have a great deal of humor.

Bob was gently teasing the little psychic, suggesting outrageous descriptions of ghosts that we were all liable to encounter. Jolly Mr. Rumford fended him off, completely good-natured about it and hoping, rather slyly, I thought, that Bob might meet one of these dead things and see for himself.

Meanwhile, in his mournful voice, the vicar said to me, "I cannot approve such devil's work." He shook his head. "Ghosts . . . Voices and apparitions of the dead . . . No. No! Not at all worthy of true Christians."

Emily put in anxiously, "But Bob was only joking. He doesn't believe in all that rubbish about creeping ghosts. He's only trying to get a raise out of poor Leander."

"Rise," said Bob.

Emily made a face at him but was far from crushed.

"Anyway, it's never happened thus far, and it isn't going to happen. We would have seen our ghosts long ago if they had actually been floating around here. What about our ancestral Duncan Calder? Surely he'd have seen ghosts if anyone did." She leaned forward earnestly, toward the melancholy vicar. "He was a dreadful man. But we aren't in the least like him."

Everyone laughed, including me. Bessie joined our laughter, a trifle late, and with a furtive little glance at her husband that may have been entirely unobserved by him, but it touched me and I thought suddenly of what I had missed in the long years since my love died in the inferno of a riddled helicopter. Curiously enough, though he smiled, Keith took his sister-in-law's hand in a gesture that warmed me.

When everyone went his way after lunch, I found myself walking out into the only modern sector of Sea Abbey in the company of the Reverend Hawkins. I tried to make small talk, but it was like blasting through the rock on which Sea Abbey was built.

"I imagine you will find the abbey very interesting. Its ancient history is considerably more—" I was about to say "lively" but the vicar didn't look as though he would appreciate liveliness in anything, above all, in ghost-ridden houses. I back-tracked quickly. "—considerably better documented than most houses of this age."

"Very true, I've no doubt." But he seemed remarkably unsure.

I tried again. "Outside these lounge windows is the only part of the island that seems to have ground. You know. Dirt, not rock."

"The rock is beneath that dirt, Madam." He pointed at the view through the end windows where the smoggy yellow light vaguely revealed the triangle of ground bravely trying to get a foot-hold in solid rock on its way down to the channel waters.

I was pretty discouraged by the Reverend Hawkins' attitude and almost ready to leave him without another word when a voice spoke behind us, subtly changing the atmosphere; for the voice was that of Keith Calder.

"Pardon me, Reverend Hawkins. Did my sister speak to you about a change in the wedding date?"

Startled, I frowned and did not greet Keith with the friendliness I had intended to display. I was about to ask if the wedding was being called off for some reason, but the quick interchange between the two men precluded that possibility.

"I really should not say, Sir. It is not my place to discuss the matter until the bride and groom have made some—er—statement."

I said suddenly, with a small laugh, "You make it sound like a police case."

"Oh, nothing like that. I may quite definitely assure you . . . That is to say, there is nothing that isn't entirely above-board in the arrangements."

Keith looked at me. His expression was serious, but I thought it was not unfriendly.

"What troubles you, Nell? Obviously, something does."

I came back almost too quickly. "The same thing that troubles you, I should think."

The vicar glanced from me to Keith and back again, anxiously.

"There seems no reason why the marriage should not be performed. Neither party—I believe I am correct in this—neither party has a previous impediment to the ceremony."

I said, "Not at that age, I hope."

"Not that I know of," Keith spoke just a second after.

I nodded.

"Then, if the young people wish to be married a few days prior to their original plan, I feel, in good conscience, that I must lend my—er—small powers to bring this about."

Keith slapped the window sill so hard we both

jumped. "All I want to know is . . . Why? Why did they advance the day? What is this hurry?"

"Really," I remarked with some amusement, "You aren't being very romantic, or even very tactful, Mr. Calder. You don't ask two young lovers why they want to be married sooner than they had planned."

"I do. They've had this date set for weeks."

"Sir!" the vicar cut in, blushing. "I am quite sure there is nothing—if you will pardon the expression—havey-cavey about this marriage. Nothing like what you obviously hint at."

Even Keith smiled. "No. I'm not hinting at anything havey-cavey."

"Because," the vicar went on nervously, "I have some recollection, from the conversation of the young people, that Miss Calder's father suggested the earlier date. Tomorrow evening. A candlelight ceremony."

I couldn't see anything suspicious about all this, but it was clear that Keith did, and that he disapproved. He had never expressed any disapproval of the wedding itself; so his sudden belligerence seemed curious, and to me, rather alarming. What did he know now that troubled him about the wedding? Or did he merely suspect something?

"So that is why you came over today with Emily and my brother," I said suddenly. "To get the marriage over and done tomorrow! I'm sure, as you say, there can't be any reason for this, except love. Nevertheless . . ."

Keith did not look at me now.

"Arrangements were perfectly satisfactory before this little trip to the mainland, to Abbeyvue. Or, at least, I heard nothing to the contrary." He added, to the obvious discomfiture of the vicar, "But perhaps the family has decided not to discuss these schemes—" He glanced my way, changed the word abruptly. "—

these plans with me. Strictly speaking, I am not one of the family."

"What was your work before you were invited to Sea Abbey?" I asked Keith, and then, realizing the indiscretion, apologized, "It is not my concern, of course."

"Not at all. I was a member of the Royal Geographic Society's study of the stratified finds in East Africa."

The vicar put in for the first time showing a spark of eagerness, "The family owes a great deal to Mister Keith Calder. When Mister Frederick Calder invited him here, Mister Keith did much to alleviate the monetary problems out of his own pocket. And as you may know, Sea Abbey is said to be expensive to keep . . . as we see it." Heaven knew how expensive it would be to restore it to its old glory!

"My ill-gotten gains," Keith explained with a faint self-mockery. "The vicar doesn't tell you they came from arms investments in the Congo. Not something that I am especially proud of."

"You shared with your fellow men. Your family," Reverend Hawkins said with what was apparently genuine pride.

But I was thinking suddenly, with my suspicious mind: "So this is why Freddie Calder and the family took in and accepted Freddie's illegitimate son! Not for love of him or for unselfish reasons at all, but because he could support them!

To tell the truth, I was still puzzled over all this fuss about the early date of the wedding. It did occur to me that if the children were married a few days sooner than originally planned, I could leave this weird island without making my departure painful to Bob, or to make it look like flight. The worst of it was, Keith seemed to read my mind.

As we left the lounge, with the Reverend Hawkins

momentarily cornered by an excited and chattering bride-to-be, Keith said to me,

"These new arrangements will at least be of help to you."

"How so?"

"You will be able to return to civilization without further journeys into Freddie's wine cellar."

"That is true. I could gladly avoid that." I hesitated. "But I will be sorry to leave the Calders, of course."

Keith looked at me briefly, but it was enough. I felt, as before, that there was more to his remarks than the mere words.

"Of course. That is the accepted politeness. I would think you a fool if you meant it. You have had a harrowing time and will be lucky to leave the abbey as soon as possible. On the other hand—" He stopped. I felt rather than heard the change in his attitude, his meaning. "I will be sorry to see you go. Sorry only for my own sake."

Curiously enough, I don't think we needed words between us to express an excitement, a warmth of feeling that had developed in these brief hours we had known each other. I suspected he was not fluent with words. When he said them, he meant them and I valued them accordingly. I did not answer him, but I felt that he understood.

Late in the afternoon, while Freddie, the lovers and Mrs. Milligan planned the scene of the wedding ceremony with the Reverend Hawkins, Mr. Rumford begged me, as a favor, to walk through every corridor, every hall and passage with him in the abbey. I was still framing a polite but definite "no" when Duncan cut in, half-joking.

"Our Nell isn't training for the Olympics, and going through these endless halls just to stir up ghosties and ghoulies is not my notion of entertainment for our fair guest."

"But it can be of vital importance, Sir. Vital! Miss Garrison has a remarkable effect on—her presence is most necessary!"

I said, "I am afraid I don't quite understand this matter of my importance. Is it a question of your being lonely, Mr. Rumford, working by yourself so much? Is that it?"

"Not at all. Not-at-all, dear lady. There are much more practical reasons. Your effect upon the crucifix on the altar last night was extraordinary. You have marvelous vibrations. Things happen near you. You are surrounded by the dead. I can almost fancy an unearthly glow around you. A thrilling thought; don't you agree?"

I looked around hastily and thanked my fates I saw nothing. I am one of those people who looks for a logical explanation to anything with the slightest touch of the supernatural. I did not want to be—as Mr. Rumford claimed—a recipient of ghostly confidences. I wanted no part in any marvelous connections between this world and the next. Assuming there was a next world.

I said, "I really am afraid I must refuse your very kind suggestion, Mr. Rumford. If you want to know the ugly truth, I'm absolutely terrified of your friends in this place. Your spiritual friends!" I added, not wanting to offend those more corporeal creatures on the island.

Duncan laughed, and slapped the psychic researcher on the back, but though Mr. Rumford tried to smile, he was clearly disappointed. As for me, I excused myself and left them in the modern half of the abbey. It was after sunset and the courtyard was shrouded in a kind of thick, yellow mist. Probably smog creeping into the usual night fog. But after Mr. Rumford's talk about those ghostly presences around me, I disliked these beginnings of darkness more than ever.

I crossed the courtyard rapidly, more rapidly than usual.

But then came the damp, ugly passage which branched off toward the tower steps and also ploughed on through that horrible, tunnel-like abbey, where I had come very close to a bad injury from that falling crucifix. I glanced at my arm in its stiff gauze dressing. A small souvenir of this place. No. I would be a fool to remain on Sea Abbey beyond the date of the wedding. And that would be tomorrow.

I stared at the long, uneven passage into the vaulted abbey's heart, that place I disliked more than any I had ever known. It was so like a grave. But there was no point in dwelling on that. I turned away from it and started up the long flights of steps. It was the hour when the out-of-doors was still light with the re-flected afterglow of dusk, and the indoors was nearly as dark as midnight. No one had yet snapped on the switch that lighted all the little, bare bulbs hung on their strings up to the level of my room. When I reached the first level, I snapped on the lights. There was apparently no one in this end of the abbey with me, and yet, when I stood still, I heard a dozen mys-terious little sounds that I could not identify.

The gentle but monotonous fall of water drops somewhere. Very slow. It was this hesitation between each drop that preyed upon my nerves. I forced my-self to smile. Bad plumbing, perhaps. Or simply the moisture from fog and channel accumulating in these ancient walls. The creak of a door gently closing seemed to trace itself much more definitely to a human being. A servant, of course.

The little shuffle of a shoe upon the abrasive surface of the steps seemed less amusing. I stopped, went back down a few steps, but saw nothing and returned to the climb toward my room. Shadows, moving subtly just beyond the periphery of my eyes, I dismissed as imaginary. When I reached my own room, I started in, then, probably because I had glanced at the wardrobe, I suddenly stepped back out into the hall, and went around to Emily Calder's room. I tried the door. It stuck momentarily and I found myself surprisingly relieved.

"Good! Remember this next time you prowl around other people's rooms," I told myself, and immediately after the door opened inward under my hand. There was nothing to do but walk in. I did so.

It was a charming room, much like that of Emily's dead grandmother, the room I was occupying. There was a little, almost junior-sized four-poster white bed complete with carefully laundered and starched white curtains. By the long French door there was an equally feminine and frilly chaise longue. I was surprised at the prevalence of old-fashioned femininity throughout the furnishings. It did not seem at all like the sort of room modern, careless Emily Calder would choose. It only went to prove that even brisk, independent, mini-skirted moderns can be romantic in private moments.

The big wardrobe was painted white as well. I hesitated, but my baser nature, or my curiosity, got the better of me and I opened the double doors in one wide, defiant gesture. There was a mirror about a foot long, hanging on the inside of the left door, and as I pushed it open, I saw, to my intense discomfort, Emily's face reflected in it behind me. At the same time, within the wardrobe, beyond the mirror, was hung my gold knit Dior suit, the sleeve badly stained and a large snag on the breast of the jacket.

EIGHT

To the reflection in the mirror I said more coolly than I felt, "Good evening, Emily. Are the wedding plans finished?"

The strange thing was that Emily looked astonished and somewhat resentful at my presence. She did not look a bit guilty. Whatever might be in that wardrobe, I was in the wrong by snooping around Emily's room, and I knew it. My question confused but by no means embarrassed her. She closed the hall door behind her. Her smile was forced, but then, so was my own.

"Nell, what on earth are you doing here? I know! you're lost. But your room is right around the corner."

I was dumbfounded at her effrontery. My fingers were already on the gold suit, about to examine the bad stains on the sleeve.

"No. I'm not lost. But thanks for the directions. This is a confusing place." I did not move away hurriedly, or apologize. I was angry at my own stupid guilt complex and meant to brazen it out just as long as she did, but unless I accused her point-blank, I couldn't keep fingering the suit sleeve forever.

She came toward me slowly, almost with deliberation, it seemed to me. For some inexplicable reason I was suddenly and briefly chilled to the bone. But I soon recovered as I continued to study her young,

leggy body and those clear eyes. But she twisted her
lower lip and sank her incisor tooth into it with a de-
termination that made me suspect she was a little
afraid of me.

"It's wonderful, Nell! Truly, it is! I adore it."

She reached into the wardrobe, took the hanger and
the suit out of my hands. She held it up against her
body, pirouetted.

"What do you think of it on me? Perfect? They
were mad about it in Abbeyvue. Bunnie MacAllister
nearly died. She knew right on that it was an import.
Only she thought it was a Chanel." She wrinkled her
short nose. "As though I wouldn't know a Dior from
a Chanel!"

"It—it looks wonderful on you, Emily." Had my
mind gone completely blank? Maybe I had given it to
her and by some mental aberration blotted it out of
my mind. It was very weird. But then, everything in
Sea Abbey was unusual. To keep from blurting out
the truth, that I hadn't the slightest idea when I gave
her a suit I had never worn, and only just had
specially made and fitted, I murmured thoughtfully,
"I have a very good little spray cleaning fluid. I use it
myself when I travel alone. May I lend it to you, to
remove the stains?"

Emily's expression lightened. The little puzzled look
vanished.

"Oh, thank you! That's so good of you! Yes, you
might give it to Mrs. Milligan or Dilys. They'll clean
my suit. Or whatever has to be done."

"A good suggestion. I'll do that." I moved away
from the wardrobe, trying hard not to let her guess
this new prick of annoyance. I had been strictly
reared, in spite of the Garrison fortune, and one lesson
I never forgot was that if I broke a toy carelessly, or
sloppily stained my clothes, I must sacrifice the toy

and I must clean off the stain. But apparently this wasn't true of the Calders.

I left her there turning this way and that, admiring herself girlishly from all possible angles. It meant a great deal to her, that suit she had so mysteriously acquired, and while I hadn't the remotest idea how she came to persuade herself I had given it to her, I was very glad she liked it so much and would not dream of trying to take it away from her.

"Nell? Don't go so fast. Nell!" She was coming after me into the hall. Still with the suit hanger in her hand—I must tell Mrs. Milligan how to take proper care of it—she rushed to hug me, squeezing both me and the suit which dragged on the floor.

"Thanks again, dear, generous sister-in-law. See you at dinner."

I returned to my room with my head whirling. I began to wonder if it was possible my brain was affected. Maybe I had a lookalike going around being more generous than I was. It was dreadfully disturbing not to be sure. Nor did it help my mental state to find myself tired and badly shaken over absolutely nothing—the silly remark of Leander Rumford that I was surrounded by ghostly manifestations, the assurance by Emily Calder that I had given her a suit worth several thousands of dollars and wasn't aware of it.

It was very dark. Darker than it would be after the moon rose. I reached over and snapped on the bed lamp in my room and lay on the bed thinking, with one arm, my good one, across my eyes.

I must have dozed off. Not surprisingly, for I was very tired, and yet I had done nothing physical today. But all the same, I felt tired in every bone, every muscle. And without being quite able to put my finger on the main problem, I realized, perhaps in my brief dream, that I was terrified for my brother's future. It was absurd. These Calders, without exception, were charming, delightful, friendly. What else could I want for Bob? I was not his mother, after all. He had his own life to live, and I would loathe a woman in my place who interfered, so I must let the wedding go through. *I could not interfere.* I would despise myself if I put any obstacle in the way of the marriage.

So what was I afraid of?

My head was pounding. I dreamed I was suffering torture at the hands of the poor monks who had been put out of their home here in the reign of Henry the Eighth. I awoke with a start. Someone was knocking on my door, and I thought it very unlikely to be one of the original, monkish owners of the abbey.

"Yes. What do you want?"

My brother Bob called, "We wondered if you were ready for dinner yet . . . my last as a single man." Apparently, Emily jolted him because his voice wavered as if he'd been hit in the ribs. He laughed and cried out: "Ooof! All right, then. My last unhappy dinner without my angel wife."

To conquer my depression I put on a particularly loud and cheerful voice.

"Hi! Good Lord! I overslept. You run on. Tell Mr. Calder . . . Freddie . . . I'll be along in just a few minutes."

"We'll wait, Nell," Emily called. "Won't we, Bobbin? We'll just wait out here, or we will be out on the upper level."

"But it's cold out there, Honey," I heard Bob protest. "You don't want an attack of flu on your wedding day."

Nevertheless, their voices faded, arguing in a light, joking way, and my spirits took a nose dive when the world around my tower room was silent again. I washed and dressed in a simple but, I hoped, suitable chiffon, found one of my new shawls, remarkably handy in this damp, cold place, and swung it over my head, drawing one end over my shoulder. I was just giving my lipstick one last touch when I felt something pale and ghostly float past my vision. Beyond the dressing table mirror was the long glass door opening onto the little balcony. I started so abruptly the lipstick cut a swathe across my cheek. I was still rubbing my cheek when I went to the door, trembling, but angry, too.

Then came the giggles, and the tapping on the door.

I had completely forgotten that Bob and Emily were going to walk out on the tiny balcony. I shook my fist at their vague, white, phantomlike faces, but I forced myself to laugh, as well. It was entirely my own fault that I had been frightened. I knew perfectly well Bob and Emily would be out there on the narrow upper level.

I was as ready now as I would ever be. I made one more swipe at my cheek with a tissue, removing what remained of the lipstick scar, although it left my cheek slightly too pink. Then I went to the French door, raised the latch, and looked out.

"Are you starved? I'm ready, at last."

The lovers were not in sight. I stepped out on the balcony. In spite of the darkness, the air was thick and yellow-gray. Not quite into deep night yet, but eerily alive with moths or perhaps it was only specks of pollution. I brushed away the fancied veil around my head, wondered if those infernal specks were tiny eyes staring at me, and then jumped a foot—almost over the low stone border—when Emily said "Boo!" in the most infantile, but amusing way.

She and Bob both grabbed at me, apologizing repeatedly, and I felt ashamed of my absurd behavior during the last few hours. Nothing more was said about Emily's newly acquired gold suit, which gave us a far more pleasant subject to dwell on at length. Emily was describing the exact, stitch-by-stitch pattern of her wedding gown which was to be delivered tomorrow morning.

"And the place for the great event! Isn't it exactly right, Bobbin? So severe and grand yet so glorious. So—medieval!"

"Not—" Surely not that ghastly vault under the tower! We were above it at this minute. I could almost feel the damp chill oozing through my thin chiffon sleeves, as I remembered that hideous vaulted tomb.

Emily hugged me, bubbling with amusement at my revulsion.

"I know you hate it, but it is terribly suitable. The splendid transept, the altar and what remains of the stained glass, and the crucifix." At my expression, she laughed once more. "And we promise not to let it fall on your head again. We'll have Father stand guard. If anybody is hit, we'll see that it is blonde Bessie."

"That's not funny, sweetheart," Bob put in a bit anxiously. "She doesn't mean it, Nell. She just talks like that."

"What do you mean, old boy? I know what I'm saying. Bessie doesn't make herself exactly well loved, you know. Always talking about money-money-money. One would think it was the only thing in life."

I could not help saying drily, "It is quite handy. At times."

"Oh, that's true! That's very true!" Emily clapped her hands and rattled on enthusiastically, "But she's not the only one in the world who has money. We're going to be so rich—after tomorrow! Aren't we, darling?"

Bob squeezed her around her lissome waist. "Don't mind Emy, Sis. She's so naive. She doesn't mean that."

"But I do!" While I laughed at her insistence, Bob managed to hush up his frank and talkative bride.

I found the walk down the steps and across the courtyard pleasant, thanks to the prospective bride and groom, whose happiness was so great I felt the contagion.

Everyone showed up at dinner except Mr. Rumford who, the Reverend Hawkins reported, was very close to "the devil's work" in his ghost hunting.

"Very near to where you and Mrs. Calder were to-day, Madam," the vicar informed me with lugubrious pride.

"What?" Bessie cried. "Well, I like his nerve! Does he think I was looking at some damned haunt or other?"

"No," said the vicar. "The courtyard wall."

Keith surprised us all by asking quietly, "What were you really looking at, Bess, when you fainted?"

She closed her mouth abruptly. I tried not to watch her, but I was still puzzled, and a little worried, over what Bessie had seen this morning. There was nothing that I could find. The most alarming thing I saw was Keith Calder's hole in the wall. Very sinister.

"Well," Bessie ventured after everyone had stared at her, obviously interested, "I—it's too idiotic."

To our embarrassment Emy said suddenly, "I knew it! You saw one of Leander's ghosts. If they pop out for my wedding, I warn you all, I shall personally exorcize them!"

Duncan laughed, Reverend Hawkins was shocked, and the rest of us changed the subject.

After the late dinner, Emily and Bob went to walk along the narrow path outside the walls and dream about their future. Duncan and Bessie, much too obviously, went off to quarrel because Bess insisted quite justly that he had not paid proper heed to her accident that morning. I saw a look in Freddie's eyes that suggested either another trek to his combined religious refuge and wine cellar or something else equally private, and I began to frame a quick excuse. Before I could say anything, however, Keith made a sign to me. Susceptible as usual to the man, I forgot about excuses, though my very susceptibility annoyed me.

"Elinor, I wish you would come with me."

"Anywhere but the vault of that dreadful tower."

He was amused, took my arm and escorted me out of the long dining room, past Freddie, who turned to the vicar with the half-hearted suggestion, "I don't suppose you would care to accompany me to the old church vault. I keep my better brandy there."

We had gone beyond hearing before I learned the reverend's answer. Regrettably, for I was curious to see if the Reverend Hawkins would fall into the trap of that haunting—and haunted?—place. My companion looked back once, as I suspected, to see what the vicar's answer would be. I smiled.

"I hope that infernal crucifix behaves better with him than with me," I remarked, and was immediately, and humorously, corrected by Keith.

"What? An infernal crucifix? Isn't that a contradiction in terms? Or are you a devil worshipper?"

"I may be. I haven't thought too much about it. Where are we going, by the way?"

"Do you mind a little mystery?"

He looked at me. I was very much aware of his fingers closed tightly upon mine. In other circumstances, I might have winced, but the pressure of his hand, like a rough lover, aroused in me only desire, not dislike.

"I don't mind at all. So long as it isn't that abbey vault." And I added, trying to soften the remark with a joke, "I only hope I can get through the wedding in there tomorrow without a calamity."

Suddenly and surprisingly angry, he said, "It was

stupid. Remarkably stupid, even for Emily. I wonder if someone—"

He broke off and I stared at him, waiting. He did not go on. It puzzled me. I wondered what he had started to say, and why he didn't finish. I tried to piece together what he had said and not said. I thought after a minute or two that he had been about to say: "I wonder if someone else persuaded her, or gave her the idea." But still, I did not know where we were going. In the modern half of the abbey, there seemed to be few enough places of interest to a man like Keith Calder.

But when we started up the steps toward the second floor, I remembered the big hole in which Keith had been working. We must be going there . . . but no! We passed the place on the landing.

I said, "Isn't this where we were going? It certainly looks sinister, this time of night."

"Why? Are you interested in the underpinnings of the house?"

I had to confess they weren't my great passion, but that I had thought there must be something about the place which he wanted me to check.

"No," he confessed, as we passed on up to the second floor. "I want you to help me with an experiment. I'm not satisfied with Bess' accident. I don't think she simply fainted. She is not a weak, Victorian female who would faint at a shadow."

Again, as earlier in the evening, fear caught at me, blotting out common sense. "What do you think happened?"

"I don't know, but I mean to find out. Do you mind?"

I said I didn't. "March on, sterling leader. I'll follow."

At least I was rewarded with his good humor and

amusement which, from a serious man, is always doubly welcome.

He snapped on the next series of hall lights and we moved rapidly along the upper hall with its narrow doors leading, I supposed, into cells like the depressing one in which I found Bessie.

"You really do have a remarkable Stately Home to add to England's collection," I said with a light note to disguise the irony. "All these rooms with their delightful southern exposure—what there is of it."

"Not a particularly nice Stately Home?" he asked, playing it lightly.

"But then, who asks to see mere nice places?"

With a kind of rueful edge to the words, he asked, "You mean—who wants to *pay* to see nice places?"

I hadn't thought of that until I finished speaking. Now, I was sorry. "I imagine it did sound as though I advocated the whole business of making money from tourists."

"It isn't an impossible notion. The Calders will have to do something soon, or go to work." As I looked at him, embarrassed over his problem, and trying to think of some way to avoid the subject, he went on with unexpected directness, "I have done what I could. But the well is running dry, I'm afraid, and it may be necessary to give up my work here, go ashore and look for a job."

"I'm so sorry. I didn't intend to bring it up. It certainly isn't my business."

He stopped. I came to an abrupt halt behind him but I had already bumped into him and he grasped my arms, making a swift, brisk apology: "Sorry!" Then, as I was disengaging myself, I found his body very close to mine, and his startling blue eyes, his lips . . .

It was a strange sort of kiss that followed. Unexpected, full of passion and surprise. He was very strong, crushingly so. And I loved him for it. For that and for other qualities.

"I lied," he confessed a trifle hoarsely when we went on.

I must have looked as startled as I felt; for he went on with a little grin, "I lied when I said I was sorry. I am not, you know."

I felt as flushed and awkward as I might have been at fifteen. I said nothing, but surely he must have guessed by my face that I, too, was not sorry.

"Here we are. The room where Bess collapsed. Would you mind playing Bess for a moment?"

I looked around the dusty little cell and started to drop to the floor.

"No! Here! You'll be covered with dust."

But if we wanted to do this thing right, re-enact the crime, so to speak, I had to drop to the floor and put myself in Bessie's collapsed position.

"How is this?" What on earth was he trying to prove? But then, I didn't really care. I only wanted to please him. And if I had to be wandering around, and lying down, in these ghastly cells, I much preferred to be in the company of Keith Calder!

He shook his head over me. I had slipped right through his arms as he tried to catch me. I was touched by his effort, but it wouldn't solve his problem. When I sprawled out on the floor as artistically as I could, he quickly accepted the situation.

"Now, let's see! When she was standing, it must have been just about—here, in order to fall in that position. What the devil could she have seen that caused her to fall?"

I looked up, getting a rather odd perspective from my position on the floor. Keith, meanwhile, went around tapping and slapping the walls, striding out into the hall and then looking back.

"If you are looking for secret passages," I said, "they went out with Mary Roberts Rinehart."

He ignored this as mere, unseemly levity. "I'd swear I can't see anything out of the ordinary."

I sat up on my elbows. "Maybe it wasn't anything out in the hall, or even—" Then I remembered the powder compact with its huge mirror. I explained about it. "Don't you think it might be something reflected? If it was anything at all, it could be an imaginary vision, a shadow . . . I saw something of that sort myself this evening. It turned out to be smog, or mist. Or whatever."

"I suppose it may have been. I can see how the lights and shadows through that window might cause some kind of illusion."

We were both startled at the sudden light and darkness as the foggy night air outside the little cell window was cut by a zooming jet.

"Something like that," we both agreed. He lifted me up, brushed me off, and with one accord we ran our fingers over the wall.

"No secret passages," he agreed. "I'm afraid there is nothing. I wish . . . never mind. It was useless, in any case." He took my arm, saw that I was amused, and belatedly realizing what he had implied, he laughed. "Sorry again for that. No. It wasn't all useless up here tonight."

I was curious to know why he was so disappointed because we hadn't found any ghosts.

"You are as bad as Mr. Rumford. Are you only happy when you are digging for ghosts?"

"Not quite. You see, I was hoping to find some logical cause for Bess' faint. If not, I am wondering why she should play out such an elaborate charade."

"As a woman, I'd say she wants to build up sympathy from her husband."

"It doesn't seem to have done its job. I'm afraid Duncan is not sentimental."

I thought that was the least that could be said of Bessie's husband, but I agreed aloud with Keith's opinion.

"You get on well together, you and your brother; though you don't have much in common. Have you always been friends?"

"Some time ago, before I came into the family, as you might say, I knew Duncan. Matter-of-fact, he introduced himself to me at a pub when I was in Bath looking over the Roman ruins. Duncan is a good fellow, in his way. Rather more like his father than I am. You must make allowances for his treatment of Bess. I'm afraid, from what I've heard, it was pretty obviously a case of buying a husband who was all too willing to be bought."

I said slowly, rather thoughtfully, "But you take an interest in her, don't you? You care what happens to her."

I knew the instant he gave me that shocked, or impatient, look that he had misunderstood me.

"I haven't the remotest interest in the woman. Not the remotest! You have only to look in your mirror, or to hear yourself, or study your own conduct, to see how far my tastes are from Bessie Calder."

Deep as my pleasure might be at the personal aspects of this confession, I felt a tiny prick of resentment on Bessie's behalf. I could not break free of the frank and straightforward realization that Bessie Calder and Elinor Garrison had a great deal in common. I explained briefly that I had meant only to praise him for his gentlemanly treatment of a fellow human being. I wanted to add that in my observation, he was almost the only one in the entire house who did treat Bessie with any courtesy.

Sometime during this conversation, Keith put hard

pressure on my hand with his thumb, and he looked down at our hands as he said now, "I pity her. But I still think she was wrong. She knew what the inducements to marriage were, and yet she . . . she bought the merchandise."

Was this a warning to me? I felt the cold dart of that truth. I must not make Bessie's mistake. Surely, he had warned me.

By the time we reached the lower floor, we came upon Mrs. Milligan, who had just finished a discussion of tomorrow's menu with the cook. She startled both Keith and me by clutching her ample bosom and crying:

"Lord, Miss Nell, you did give me a turn! Whatever are you doing here in the new abbey?"

Keith frowned, glanced at me. "Why shouldn't she be here? We've been examining the room where Mrs. Calder fainted this morning."

"Oh, but everyone thought you had gone to your room. I beg pardon, I'm sure. I was that took aback, I thought you might be one of that Mr. Rumford's hobgoblins. He's a wicked man, is that one! I don't hold with High Church, being of the Roman faith myself, but this I'll say! The reverend's right about it being a sin to conjure up ghosts and the like."

"I wonder, Mrs. Milligan—" I began when I could get a word in, "—if you could tell me who said I was going to my room. Who said it first?"

Both Keith and Mrs. Milligan were curious. "Does it matter?" he asked, obviously voicing her question.

"Well, I'm afraid I don't know, Ma'am. It was one of those mixed-up things. Let me see now. I was asking for the wedding list. How many to sit down at dinner . . . no guests, as it happens . . . there was coming in and going out. I never paid too much notice. I spoke to Miss Emy. And sometime along there, Mr. Duncan was having words with his wife. And then he had words with Mr. Rumford about digging right where Mr. Rumford's haunts were. Really, Ma'am—Sir—my mind was that busy, I couldn't give you any closer guess."

"You're right. It really doesn't matter. Thank you so much. I think I will turn in now. We have a good deal to look forward to tomorrow."

"Not the least of which is Emy's mini-skirt wedding gown," Keith joked as we left the puzzled Mrs. Milligan.

We started across the courtyard under those high, milky globes when the lights went out. Shortly after, from the modern building we had just left, came a shriek of anguish and profanity from Bessie Calder.

"Damn!" Keith said, and then explained rapidly, "We have a wholly inadequate plant. These lights are on a circuit with those in the modern building. Poor Bess! She hates the darkness, and here she is, caught in the middle of it."

I saw that the light was still on in Bob's room on the lower lever of the ancient tower.

"I think I'll go on then, if you don't mind. The step lights are still on, I hope, in the old building."

"Yes. They're a different circuit. Older, but more reliable. I'd rather take you to your room, but this seems to be a crisis."

He insisted on escorting me through the half-dark of the courtyard to the tower entrance, however. We stood there briefly in the night that was illuminated only by the thick, foggy sky and that one bar of light from Bob's room above us. I could see Keith's eyes, intense and, to me at least, remarkably bright. He let my hand go. It was like the release from a friendly vise. Then we went in opposite directions, I up the stone steps, blinded momentarily by the little string of naked lights. Busy thinking of Keith, I found the climb to the upper level surprisingly short.

Nevertheless, when I came to the little hall which led to my room, my steps slowed. As always, I felt the curious crowding of centuries around me, the oppressive sense that all those monks chased out of their ancient quarters by a king's greed were watching me now. I opened the door, felt for the light switch, meanwhile imagining that I saw a huddled black mass on the floor between the French door and my night stand. The lamplight glowed suddenly, casting a soft pink patina over the room.

And over the huddled black mass which was the Reverend Hawkins lying dead upon my floor.

NINE

It must have been several very long minutes before I persuaded myself that the poor man actually lay there on the floor, and that he was dead. My brain and imagination had it so fixed that he was a mere shadow, something conjured up in my mind, that I could hardly absorb the hideous fact. He did not seem to be wounded in any way. It must have been a sudden attack. Heart, probably. And small wonder, if he had climbed all those steps to the upper level!

But what in heaven's name was the Reverend Hawkins doing in my room?

The water glass that usually stood on my night stand had fallen to the floor, probably shaken off by the impact of the vicar's body. I started to pick up the glass, thought better of it, and left it there. I was not suspicious over his death. There was obviously no foul play. There wasn't a mark on his face or hands, nor blood on his threadbare black suit. But I decided not to touch anything. It seemed the sensible thing.

I hurried out to Emily's room. The door was locked from the inside. I had to knock several times and finally call to her. She opened the door a few inches, scowling, dripping wet, and wearing a tiny terrycloth robe.

"What the bloody hell is it, Dilys? Oh, it's you, Nell! 'Scuse the drips. I was tubbing away and dreaming of tomorrow." Her frown dissolved into her usual bubbly self. "Guess why?"

"Emily—" I hated to see all that cheerfulness shadowed. With the wedding so close it seemed a shame that all her plans must be blown sky-high. "I'm sorry, but I'm afraid there's been an accident. There isn't a phone here, is there?"

"Not in these rooms. Why?" Her still-damp hands grabbed me painfully. "Not Bobbin. Oh, God! Not Bobbin!"

"No, no. Nothing like that. We'll have to get him, though. It's the vicar. I think he is dead."

Completely confused, she made me repeat this. "How do you know? Where is he? In the courtyard? Did you see him from up here?"

"He is in my room. Why, I've no idea. Maybe he wanted to talk to me. Can you get Bob now, please? And then the family."

"Of course." She started blindly out in the hall, got a chill on her bare flesh, and rushed back inside. In less than a minute she was thoroughly wrapped in a floor-length velour robe, her wet hair dripping down her back. Her teeth were chattering but she said valiantly, "I'm r-ready."

My own knees felt weak and I understood perfectly when we reached my room why Emily retreated behind me, murmuring apologetically, "I n-never saw a man dead b-before. They never asked me to see Mother. I was too young. And Granny . . . I could never look at Granny. But is that really poor Mr. Hawkins? He looks exactly as though he might be asleep; doesn't he?"

I paid little attention to these ramblings but examined the vicar again, more carefully. There were still no signs of injury except that the skin on his palms was a little rubbed, as if the vicar had put his hands out to protect himself when he fell.

I said, "Go and call Bob, please. And then get one of your brothers. Or both."

She started, then remembered something. She crossed the room, meticulously stepping over the Reverend Hawkins' body to get to the glass door. She looked out. "It's going to be hard. The lights are still out over there." She turned back to me, clasping her hands tightly. "What'll we do, Nell? I don't wander around this old place in the dark. I never did."

Impatient and nervous, I said crossly, "Well, then, send Bob with a flashlight."

Carefully, she stepped back over Reverend Hawkins and went out into the hall, grumbling. "I had to talk and talk to get that silly man here to the island. And now he's gone off and died. He wasn't that old!"

"Please, hurry!"

She disappeared along the hall. I heard her feet clattering girlishly down the worn and sloping steps. I was left with the unfortunate vicar. I began to wonder if he was actually dead. I touched him in a gingerly way, checked his thin wrist for a pulse. Nothing. I stood up, studying the French door and the thick, foggy night pushing against the glass. I went over to the balcony door, walking around the Reverend Hawkins, and opened the door.

Out on that shadowed, incredibly narrow balcony, I tried to make out something human in the courtyard far below. I kept thinking, not of the luckless Reverend Hawkins, but of the grand old lady of the Calder family who had tumbled off this low balcony to her death in that courtyard which looked, at this hour, deceptively soft, deceptively pale and padded with fog.

Apparently Keith was still having trouble with the lighting in the modern sector of the abbey. I saw that great, gray hulk beyond the courtyard in which there were flaring lights which appeared and disappeared, along with the steady glow of what obviously were flashlights. I hoped and prayed that someone would appear. A servant? Someone.

It seemed an age but probably was five minutes before I saw my brother Bob running across the courtyard toward the modern half of the abbey. Before he entered the new sector, he met someone whom I recognized with relief as that small, compact Mrs. Milligan. She heard his story briefly, glanced up at the tower where I stood.

"Please come up," I called to her.

She nodded in the glow of Bob's flashlight and with a quick wave at me indicating, I hoped, that she would join me, she bustled across the courtyard. I was so glad of her help, anyone's help, that I turned abruptly to go inside. A great, white thing floated past me, clinging to my face, hideous and terrifying. I wavered, tearing at the thing which dissolved in my fingers . . .

A newspaper. Nothing but a newspaper! It had been caught on a current of air and swept past me. Accidentally? Or was this something planned by a malignant mind?

What was it doing up here? Where had it come from? An instant more, a step closer to the edge, and in my panic I would have plunged over like the woman who had occupied this tower room before me. Badly shaken, I leaned against the wall of the tower while I caught my breath and regained my equilibrium. In a very gingerly way I peered in through the glass door and saw the dead man. Gleaming in the lamplight was the water glass from which I always drank before I slept. It lay just beyond the outstretched fingers of the dead man's right hand.

Absently, I reminded myself that I must have another water glass before I slept tonight. Not that I would sleep here. A few minutes later and I might have drunk from that glass.

Now, why did I think of that? Was there something wrong with the glass? For one thing, a dead man had drunk from it. Or rather, a man had drunk from it before he died.

"Nell! Where are you?" Emily called.

Furtively, not understanding my own secretiveness, I watched her come into my room, look around, and then stare long and hard, with a certain revulsion, at the Reverend Hawkins. I waited. She looked up, called me again, and hearing nothing, moved toward the door, stepping over the dead man with a kind of youthful "It can't happen to me" insouciance that I envied.

It was clammy with fog outside and I was just about to reveal my whereabouts when Emily pressed her face against the glass. I wondered what her thoughts were. She looked positively sinister, her nose and lips nastily flattened by the glass. She looked down. Did she expect to see me at the bottom of the tower, all my bones broken in my fall?

Shocked at my own momentary suspicions, I stepped forward directly into her vision. Her peculiar expression, neither horrified nor particularly indicative of any other emotion, slowly softened. I hoped the look she gave me was one of relief. She opened the door, let me in.

"Take care. Don't want to step on the poor chap."

"No," I agreed rather flatly. "I think he's suffered rather more than his share at Sea Abbey."

She ignored that. "You're shaking."

"It was cold out there."

She seemed puzzled. "What on earth were you doing out there at this hour?"

"Trying to see if anyone in the other building knew we were alive . . . some of us, that is."

She grinned, then quickly sobered. "Sorry. I don't like being here with—him."

I nudged her over to the chair by the door. She sat down, shaking quite as much as I, while I went out into the hall and called down the steps to Mrs. Milligan.

Mrs. Milligan may have been shocked at the tragedy, but she was much more occupied with her breathless climb as she came into sight, a most welcome sight with all her staunch and normal solidity. No ghost was Mrs. Milligan!

"Dearie me!" she exclaimed, fanning herself with a delicate lawn handkerchief. "That *is* a climb. Now then, is it a certain thing he's dead?"

I nodded. For some reason I found myself choked with feeling for the poor young vicar. A good man, a well-intentioned man in a noble calling; yet he lay there dead, with all his good deeds or well-meaning efforts come to nothing.

Mrs. Milligan peered at Reverend Hawkins while Emily and I stared at her anxiously. She went down on one knee, creaking just a little, and as her blunt, useful fingers went over his body and head, she looked over her shoulder at us.

"If I don't make too bold, Miss Elinor, what business had the man with you in your room, and so late? Not—" she added modestly, "—that it's properly a question I've the right to ask."

"Please," I said, "you've every right. I'm sure it's a puzzle to everyone on the island. Including me. I don't think we've exchanged ten words since he arrived. I came up here half an hour ago, and turned on the light and found him here."

Emily broke in thoughtfully, "That's what I don't understand. What was he doing so far from the guest room where we put his poor old valise?"

"Could he have lost his way, come too far up the

steps, and then the exertion was too much for his heart?" It was only a half-hearted suggestion and I didn't expect anyone to welcome it with open arms, but both Emily and Mrs. Milligan crushed it together. Mrs. Milligan was almost shocked.

"Oh, no! The reverend was put in the new building, near Mr. and Mrs. Duncan's suite."

"Lord, no!" Emily cut in at the same time. "Only special people get in the tower. This is historic, you know."

I assumed they were telling me I was specially blessed with the tower room.

The housekeeper, having run her hands over the vicar's body and found nothing to indicate the cause of his death, got up and brushed her hands briskly.

"It'll take a man to be more precise about it," she explained with delicate emphasis. "I expect it was the climb, all the same, atop that heavy dinner the poor soul ate. What I'm thinking is, Ma'am, he might've wanted a word with you in private, and he made the climb and then fell dead."

"Millie, what nonsense!"

Nonsense was an old-fashioned word and I glanced at Emily, but she seemed very much in earnest. I, on the contrary, began to think very favorably of Mrs. Milligan's suggestion. At the moment, though, there was a matter of much greater urgency.

"You think then, that it was his heart?" I asked Mrs. Milligan, because she seemed a straightforward, intelligent witness to call in at such a moment.

"Very like. But it does seem odd. Coming up here to—well—"

I felt like a Sadie Thompson, who had enticed the unfortunate vicar up to my room for highly sensual reasons. I was about to explain again when, to my intense relief, we heard male voices on the steps and someone opened the hall door which the housekeeper had left ajar. I told myself that I might have known it would be Keith Calder who got here first, to help, and to take over when the rest of us hadn't the slightest idea of what to do.

Behind him clambered Duncan and Bob. It was my brother who asked me while Keith was examining the dead man, "Nell! Are you all right? Don't let it get you down, Sis. He must have been exploring and he got winded and just . . . dropped dead of exhaustion. Don't you think so, Keith?"

"Hm," said Keith noncommittally. He looked up at me. "You're looking very pale. You mustn't hang about here worrying, wearing yourself out. Emily, you and Mrs. Milligan find Elinor a decent room where she can have a little peace and quiet. Dunc, pack some things for her. And while you are in the other building, explain the whole affair to Freddie, if he isn't off with Rumford hunting brandy and ghosts."

Mrs. Milligan said, "Excuse me, Sir, but Mister Freddie knows all about it. He went to call Mr. Rumford."

"Hadn't we better call the police, or whoever?" I suggested. "Someone on the shore?"

Keith smiled faintly. "Quite right. There is a telephone system of sorts in the other building. Call the Abbeyvue constable, Dunc."

"What the devil do I say, old man? There's been a death? Someone climbed the stairs too fast?"

Before Keith could answer this callous remark, Emily surprised me by crying out, "Don't be so God-damned rotten about it. Haven't you any feelings at all?"

"I have that," Duncan told her a bit hoarsely as they wrangled in one corner while I helped Keith turn the dead man over. "It's just that it makes things damnably easier if you don't make a deal of fuss."

All of us except the brother and sister were trying without result to discover if there was any evidence that the reverend died of unnatural causes. Keith shook his head finally, reached over and took my hand.

"You're cold as ice. You shouldn't be hanging about here. Emy! Do as I told you!"

Everybody looked a little frightened. As for me, I could not remember when, since that helicopter went down long ago, any man had spoken of me with this concern, this passionate care for my welfare. Emily and I took with us a nylon gown and peignoir, some lingerie and another pair of shoes.

"And a sleeping pill," I said. Everyone looked at me. I explained quickly. "Only one. Don't worry. I seldom take them, but I'm pretty shaky tonight."

I suppose they dubbed me one of those pill-taking Yankees, but I couldn't help that. I really was badly shaken.

"Where do you keep them?" Duncan asked as he rummaged through the wardrobe, an absurd place for pills.

I reached into the drawer of the night stand, found the little prescription box and took it out. Almost absently, I rattled it as I started to drop it into my handbag. No answering rattle! I opened the box. Everyone stopped what he was doing and stared at the open box in my hand. It was empty. For a minute I simply looked at it with a small surprise. But I knew what the others were thinking. "A compulsive pill-taker! Doesn't even know how many she takes!"

"That's funny. I haven't taken one for a couple of weeks, but I know I had ten or eleven capsules left. The box must have come open in the drawer."

And closed by itself?

Nor was there any capsule rolling around free in the drawer.

"Well, they're gone now!" Duncan made the obvious observation. Then he shrugged and started to take my clothes out of Emily's arms when I reminded him.

"Emily can't go. She's only just gotten out of the tub. She isn't even dressed for it. She'll catch cold."

"I'm perfectly warm," she insisted with Bob's arm around her, but though the velour robe looked cozy and attractive, her teeth were chattering and Bob backed up my insistence that she should "hop into bed before you get pneumonia and call off our day tomorrow." Then he remembered, flushing a little as he looked at the dead vicar, and apologized in a low voice. But I'm sure no one could blame him or Emily if, so close to their wedding, they could not keep their minds on the tragedy of the young vicar's death.

Keith glanced at his young half-sister who, aside from being nearly as shaken as I must look, was also cold, with a fear that I thought she tried gallantly to play down.

"Elinor is right. Emy, go to bed and wrap up. Duncan—no. Bob, will you and Mrs. Milligan take Elinor to some decent room—a warm, dusted room. None of Bess' haunted cells, Mrs. Milligan."

"No, indeed, Sir! As if I would!"

I wondered why he changed his mind and did not send his brother with me. Perhaps he feared an explosion from Bessie. Yes. It must be that. It couldn't be, a nasty thought prompted me, that he wanted to keep only the Calders around him when the police were called. What would be the point? There was nothing to hide. So far as we could tell, there were no marks of violence on the dead man.

I started away with my brother, who took my things, and with Mrs. Milligan, who looked excited, probably nervous, but also her efficient self.

"It does set a problem," she murmured after looking back once at the body. We went down the steps, Mrs.

Milligan leading the way, and Bob behind us. Then the housekeeper seemed to find an answer to one of her problems. "There'll be the room Mister Duncan uses when he's had words with Mrs. Bessie. It's right next to their suite. But no connecting doors. You'll have your privacy. I'm afraid you'll have to use the bathroom next to the lounge though, if it's all the same to you, Miss."

"Yes, of course. I'm so sorry to put you to all this bother. I probably could have stayed in that room. It was very pleasant, until—"

Bob cut in angrily, "Don't be ridiculous, Nell! You wouldn't sleep ten minutes without remembering that poor devil lying there."

"Not a devil, Sir. Hardly a devil. Though he *was* High Church!"

I don't think Bob understood Mrs. Milligan's perfectly sober, if absurd, remark. He went on with the puzzle that occupied us all. "The queerest thing about it is—what was he doing there in the first place?"

We were descending the last flight of steps to the ground floor and that grim, damp pathway to the church altar, and Mrs. Milligan was a little winded. She pressed a hand to her solid bosom and said matter-of-factly, "He must've wanted to speak, private-like, with Miss Nell. Would you not say so, Ma'am?"

"Very likely."

"But about what?" Bob asked. "That's the crazy thing."

Just as Mrs. Milligan set one foot flatly and firmly on the uneven stone floor at the bottom of the steps, she screamed. This threw me into a panic and undoubtedly, Bob too, but he managed to control himself better.

"What's going on? What happened?"

Something seemed to materialize out of the

shadows, and because of the housekeeper's short stature, it loomed above her, until we recognized Freddie Calder's smooth, unctuous voice.

"Ah, here you are. Everything all taken in hand? Trust old Keith for that. My dear Nell! What a shock for you! But the poor beggar never was very strong, you know. I suspect he took the wrong turn on those infernal steps. He must have intended to visit the bridegroom here for a little pre-nuptial advice."

"Me!" Bob laughed shortly. "I don't know what advice he thought I needed at my age." For the first time in hours I felt amused. Clearly, Bob was affronted for fear someone might suspect he didn't know his way around sexually. But Freddie explained in his usual, easy way.

"You know the advice. Be kind. Be understanding. Be the perfect spouse. Very commonplace nowadays. Where are you going, Mrs. Milligan?" The housekeeper was headed toward the courtyard entrance, which was still exceedingly dark. "Leander personally suggested he give up his room to Nell, so she won't have to be routed out across that cold, dark courtyard."

"I can't do that, Mr. Calder. I can't take Mr. Rumford's room."

"We insist upon it. Leander's got a notion tonight he will hear from his dead friends in the church vault. Something to do with poor Hawkins' demise. Hawkins is, I believe, to serve as Leander's guide to—well, wherever he expects to meet his ghosts. Not my dish of tea, I'm afraid. In any case, Leander has taken a mattress. Going to sleep beside the altar. In there." He gestured behind him toward that long, hideous tunnel.

I could not think of anything more horrible. If given the choice, I would rather have slept in the same room as the Reverend Hawkins' dead body! I said, "I sincerely hope the crucifix is anchored down."

But Freddie insisted it was Leander's wish; so I thanked him, and asked him to convey my appreciation to Mr. Rumford.

"Where is his room?" Bob asked.

I was somewhat less than comfortable when I learned that the door—surely five or six hundred years old—was behind the stone steps and only a few feet away from that tunnel-like passage into the heart of the abbey, and its gloomy church altar. This was almost going from bad to worse, yet I could make no objections. Heaven knows, the Calders had enough to contend with that night! In the dim light of a single small globe, Bob and I exchanged looks and Bob started to say something. I shook my head, but he wasn't happy about it.

"You and I will trade," he suggested as Mrs. Milligan pulled the door open. It was too heavy and too warped to work inward. But I refused his offer firmly. What I really wanted to do was get through the night as quickly and with as few complications as possible. I would make other plans, leave Sea Abbey, after the wedding tomorrow.

But there could be no wedding now!

I'm sure the others around me shared my anxiety to have me settled and out of everyone's way. I stepped into the room. Rather, I stepped down into a medieval chamber. The stone floor had sunk in a way that would shock an antequarian. The stones seemed to roll up and down like the floor of Venice's St. Mark's, and gave the viewer a decidedly seasick sensation. Not that the room was terrifying, or ugly. It was magnificent. Except that the glorious purple velvet bed curtains were badly worn, almost threadbare, and the long velvet drapes at the window were sun-streaked, and although the enormous room had been swept and dusted, it still looked as if one of those ancient monks might float out of the shadows at any moment. What an ideal home for Leander Rumford's ghosts!

Bob watched me worriedly.

"It's marvelous!" I cried with every ounce of enthusiasm I could muster. "I've never seen such a place! That is—" They were all looking at me. "—it should be a museum."

"Yes. That's the thing to do with it," Bob agreed flatly.

In the end, however, I persuaded him to put my clothes down and go, along with Mrs. Milligan and Freddie. Once again, I apologized for taking Mr. Rumford's room, but this was courteously waved aside, and they all left. There was no lock on the door. The latch itself proved to be useless, but the stones were so uneven I would certainly hear any intruder who unwisely ventured in. In fact, just to open the door, I had to push hard and then grit my teeth against the awful grating screech that echoed through the passage.

I satisfied myself that the huge bed, big enough to accommodate at least three pairs, was free of spiders and dust. Then I bathed in the tiny bathroom which was obviously an afterthought to the chamber. I was very tired, but almost too tired to rest; so I walked around the gigantic chamber, examining the room's furnishings, and half-heartedly looking for secret passages, which I failed to find among the high stone walls. I even peeked and poked behind the tapestries, so thread-bare I could almost see through them, but found nothing any more dangerous than mold.

At the same time, my mind kept reverting to the vicar's death.

When I returned to the bed and climbed in, actually mounting three steps, I looked around with a sigh for the glass of water I usually drank, and also for the sleeping pill that, for once, might have proved useful.

It was curious, I thought, that the dying man had pulled my water glass over when he fell. He must have drenched the carpet and himself.

But, of course, he didn't drop the glass full of water. There was no water stain around anywhere. What had happened to it? Perhaps it hadn't been poured for me yet.

Then I sat straight up in bed. It seemed preposterous that I hadn't thought of it before. All my sleeping pills had been in their little box when I put them in the drawer. Someone had taken them.

And had that person emptied the capsules into my glass of water, knowing the vile taste of chemical treatment would cover the act? If so, then, theoretically, I was the dead person on that floor. Poor Reverend Hawkins, breathless and thirsty, had drunk the poisoned water meant for me.

TEN

Eventually, I slept and remained in deep, undisturbed sleep, or so I thought, until I was awakened by the furious screech of the door being opened. It was still dark. I could make out nothing. I fumbled for the lamp, remembered too late that there was only one electric light in the room, and that one was overhead. I would have to get out of bed to snap on the switch.

"Who is it?" I called out, frightened, but angry, too. I half expected some weird, floating thing which would not, of course, answer me. I was enormously relieved when the intruder spoke straight out in Keith's voice. I was learning to love that voice as I loved the man. Clearly impossible when I had barely known him two days. And too, there was Bess Calder's warning, the lesson of her own fate in being desired for her money.

"Elinor, this is Keith. I heard you scream. Are you all right?" He snapped on the light. I blinked, and like a schoolgirl, reached for my black nylon peignoir, a wholly inadequate covering. He himself was still fully dressed. Had he been up all night? If so, had he spent this time working on the mystery of the vicar's death? I wondered if he or the other Calders had ever notified the shoreside police.

"I didn't scream. . . . Or—I suppose it must have been a nightmare. Did I really scream?"

124

"I'm afraid so. I was just returning from the church altar when I heard you. But you are all right?"

"Good heavens! You went into that place at this hour? I don't envy you."

He smiled. "You forget I'm quite used to it. I've done a good deal of exploring in there since I came to Sea Abbey."

I shivered. "But at this hour!"

"Only to see how Leander was doing."

So he was worried about that place as much as I!

"From your manner I assume he was doing very well."

"Snoring away. I'm afraid he won't see anything tonight, even if the place comes alive with apparitions."

I didn't see how the little man could sleep at all. At the same time I wasn't too anxious for him to be successful in his quest.

"They won't come floating past this little hall bedroom, I hope."

He approached the bed, which meant that he took about six long paces, hands clasped behind him, and was still separated from this enormous bed by what appeared to be half a mile. The amused gleam that softened his face was gone. His mouth was hard, his eyes concerned.

"It was a dream . . . wasn't it? Tell me the truth. Don't spare us in order to be polite."

"It must have been a dream. I do remember the unpleasantness of it. One of those 'walking-through-a-long passage' things." I tried to smile, to keep him from thinking of me as a kind of mill-stone around the Calder necks. "But your family is not responsible for my nightmares. I mean—it wasn't your fault that the vicar climbed all those steps, drank a glass of water, and died."

I caught my breath. I had intended to keep this

knowledge to myself for a time. And now, if my voice gave any indication of irony, he might guess what I suspected.

Unfortunately, he did suspect. He came on to the foot of the bed, clasped the nearest bedpost in a hand whose knuckles were white with tension.

"What about this glass of water? Was there some significance in it for you?" He saw from my face that his tone had startled me and then he further startled me by slapping the bedpost. "I beg your pardon. I had no right to talk to you as though you were—"

"What?"

He stood there looking at me for a long and embarrassing time. Then he shifted his gaze. He was not a man to mince words, and it shook me emotionally when, in his abrupt way, he said, "Why couldn't you be plain Elinor Smith?"

I couldn't help laughing at this non-sequitur. "It is impossible for me to be Smith, because my mother married a man named Garrison. It works that way in the States."

But this didn't have the intended effect. Perhaps he thought I was needling him about his own illegitimacy, which hadn't even occurred to me until I finished speaking. He did not look around and I could only guess from his voice that he was still exceedingly serious.

"Money! It can be the biggest barrier in this damned world!"

"Lack of money is said to be uncomfortable, too," I reminded him. I said this on a small, teasing note, but he didn't react properly. He turned to me, said with considerable force, "Yes! In this house it amounts to an obsession! There are times when I wish to God I'd never seen the Calders!"

I was still fumbling for words to soothe this complex character when he walked out of the room—

without another word. It was an exit that demanded the slamming of a door, but the door to this medieval chamber was un-slammable. He pushed it open. It screeched throughout the lower floor of the abbey, and his figure seemed to dissolve into the darkness beyond.

It took me some time to recover from this encounter. I remembered how he looked at me, the hard slap of his hand against the bedpost, the furious—and passionate?—way he wished I could be Elinor Smith. My flesh yearned for his touch, but I could still lie there with the tingling sense of his presence, long after he was gone.

"I guess this is the real thing for you, old girl!" I told myself. "You don't fall in love easily. But Keith Calder is the One." And this in spite of the fact that Bessie was probably right when she warned me that my money was an obstacle. The difference being that it was not quite an obstacle in the way that Bessie had prophesied.

After getting up and snapping off the light, I slipped down under the covers, enjoying the feel of the soft, worn, but well-laundered sheets and trying not to think of how old the blankets were. Keith, in his haste to leave, hadn't closed the door tightly, and once I had gotten into bed and tried to sleep, the knowledge of that partially opened door haunted me. I stared at it, or where I thought it ought to be, for a long time, hoping that when I did sleep, I wouldn't arouse myself, or any other person in the abbey, by some wild nightmare scream. Unfortunately, I was less ready for sleep now than I had been some minutes ago, before Keith came in to disturb me.

I must have tried for nearly an hour to get back to sleep, hearing—or imagining I heard—dozens of strange noises suggestive of prowling creatures. I lay in that great bed and shook. I was very nearly, though not quite, reduced to pulling the covers over my head. Finally I dozed off.

This time I was awakened by regular footsteps, heavy and shuffling, on stonework somewhere near. The articles of furniture in the big chamber were faintly visible in a blurred gray light. It must have been shortly before dawn. I heard the sounds so persistently I finally got up, threw the useless peignoir around me, and went to the huge door. It had stuck open on the uneven stones, and I squeezed through without pushing it open further.

I moved silently, like a conspirator, around from the back to the front of the steps. I was just in time to see the trousers and feet of two men who certainly didn't appear to be members of the household. Above them, I could hear Keith's voice.

"But we haven't moved him. We examined—that is, I examined him. And I believe our housekeeper, Mrs. Milligan, and Miss Garrison, whose room this is. But no one else. We turned him over. Later, I stripped him and then dressed him, enough for decency. The poor devil deserved that, at least. But I couldn't find a wound."

"Heart, Sir. Most likely. A deal of that going about," one of the unknowns volunteered.

It was very cold. Clammy cold in that passage at the foot of the steps with the open archway into the courtyard nearby. After satisfying myself that these were police and perhaps a doctor or coroner, I hurried back to the big medieval chamber, hugging my arms against the cold. I got back into bed, huddled there until I stopped shaking.

It was after sunrise when the same feet came shuffling down, this time heavier than before. They were carrying a load. I closed my eyes, trying to think of other things. But with the selfishness of most human beings, I couldn't help thinking: except for mere chance, they could be carrying my body down those steps. If the Reverend Hawkins had died of the powder from those capsules, then that glass of water was meant for me.

And if so, who had prepared the glass?

The progression of ideas was too horrible. I lay there with my mind whirling. I knew better than to try and force all this out of my mind. As a result, and somewhat to my own surprise, I went off to sleep. I did dream, but only of the most harmless matters. And finally, of Keith Calder. A Keith Calder with no scruples about living with me in spite of my money. I awoke at the moment I was becoming suspicious that maybe it was the money, after all, that attracted Keith. This time, although I considered it a nightmare, no one heard me scream.

As I lay there dreading my morning encounter with the possibly murderous Calders, I heard the bright, unbearably cheerful notes of Leander Rumford's voice.

"A near-run thing, Mrs. Bessie. A very near thing. Had I awakened a minute earlier, I believe I might have seen the ectoplasmic manifestation of the poor reverend's soul. I shall know better when I have examined the precise spot where the—er—calamity occurred. Not that I would regard such a mere passing from one plane to another as a calamity. But I daresay, the reverend may have been of two minds about it."

"The reverend," Bessie reminded him tartly, "didn't believe in any of your fool ectoplasm. And if he'd had his voice, I don't doubt he'd a great deal rather you had met the calamity, as you call it, than him. Can't say as how I blame him, when it comes to that."

Mr. Rumford apparently started into the room where I had slept, because a new voice cut in suddenly. Mrs. Milligan called out from a distance,

"No, no, Rumford! Excuse me. Miss Garrison's sleeping in your room. With your permission, the way I heard it. Here's her morning tea. Will you be standing out of my way, Sir?"

"Nice business all around," Bessie remarked while I sat up quickly, trying to do something with my tangled, dishevelled hair.

When Mrs. Milligan came in, I welcomed her with open arms, figuratively speaking. She tried to look suitably depressed over the tragedy, but her cheerful, chubby face could not so easily fall into negative lines.

"And how did you sleep, Miss Elinor? No more awful things happening right under your very nose, I hope."

"No. Thank you. Have they come about Mr. Hawkins?"

"Come and gone. Poor soul. Now then, you'll be after warming yourself. This is a perfect fridge of a room."

"You are a blessing, Mrs. Milligan!"

"It's the tea does the trick, every time. Nice, dark tea, dark as that foul coffee you'll all be drinking in the States. It's the peat you see. Makes all the difference how the water's boiled."

She set the tray on my lap and it was so welcome I forgot washing, baths, the investigation of the vicar's death, forgot everything but Mrs. Milligan's peat-tasting tea. I had already poured the tea—it really was dark as coffee!—and drunk one scalding mouthful, when Bessie Calder stuck her head in.

"You can go, Milligan. I'll take over."

I thanked the housekeeper and put a hand out to her gratefully. She took it with surprise and a friendly grin. Almost before she had gone, Bessie was saying to me loudly, in confidence,

"That old biddy acts like she owns this crummy heap personally."

I said frankly, "Maybe that is why I feel more at home with her than with the Calders."

But somewhat to my surprise, Bessie Calder wasn't the least offended. At any rate, if she was, she concealed it admirably. She came over to the bed, studied it, remarked, "Dunc would like this bed. He's such an elephant, he needs this much room." She punched the mattress with her fist, just missing my feet. In spite of my annoyance at her remark about Mrs. Milligan, she put me in good humor again.

I asked if this huge bedchamber was ever used, except by ghost-hunting guests like Leander Rumford.

"Oh, no, Keith sleeps here now and again. But nobody else would have it."

"Not enough room, I take it."

This went completely over Bessie's blonde head. I asked if she had heard a physician's report on the cause of the vicar's sudden death.

"Not yet. Heart, everyone says."

She shrugged, then went over to the ancient, dark-armoire, against a far wall, and opened it.

"Mind if I look over the wardrobe of our Yankee Dollar Princess?"

I felt like asking her if I might see the wardrobe of a British Pound Princess, but didn't quite have the nerve. In the end I went into the icy-cold little bathroom which must once have been a torture chamber, and bathed and wrapped myself in the man-sized terry cloth robe hanging there. When I came out, Bessie was holding up to herself the *Pake* style Chinese dress Emily had selected for Bob to take downstairs from the room on the upper level.

Bessie said calmly, "You shouldn't have given that gold bit of fluff to Emy. This'n's not half so fine."

"Who—who told you about the suit?"

"My husband, of course. When he told me you gave it to him for Emily, I thought you were crazy. Now, I'm sure of it."

. . . I ought to have done it without Duncan's intervention, I thought. By this time, I knew the presents I had brought for the bride, while more valuable, would not be nearly as much valued as a wardrobe from the French *Haute Couture*. Well, it wasn't too late. If Bob would not resent it as interference, I could see that she got her clothes.

But in spite of all these thoughts, way down deep, I did resent Duncan's easy purloining of what was not his own property.

In spite of Bessie's opinion of the padded Chinese dress with its high tight collar and split skirt, I put it on and felt comfortable and warm on what looked likely to be a wet, sloppy day. She, meanwhile, was walking around the room, following the stone walls.

"Bloody awful place, I'll say that." She would have done some more complaining, apparently aware of difficulties beyond those I had noticed, but we were both startled by Leander Rumford's heavy knock on the partially opened door. He managed to make it sound like the Beethoven Victory notes.

I motioned to him. "Please come in. Thank you so much, Mr. Rumford, for loaning me the room."

"Had a good sleep, eh, Miss Garrison? Any visitors in the night?"

I started, wondering if he knew about Keith's visit in the middle of the night. "I'm sure if there were any visitors, that door would announce them to the world."

"But, dear lady! Not through this door. Through what we laughingly call the secret passage."

"I knew it!" I cried. "I knew there had to be one, and if there were one, I would have to receive it. Do you mean to tell me they let me sleep here all night with secret passages all over the place?" I started for the armoire. "Not another minute in this ghastly dungeon!" I had my hands full of my night things and a sport coat before either Bessie or Leander could stop me.

"You don't look like a bloody coward, Nell!"

"Well, I am!"

"Miss Garrison!" That was Leander Rumford. "It was only a bit of a joke. See? Nothing, really."

Nothing? The sinister thing was just behind the head of the bed, concealed by the bed hangings. I went back and examined it. The narrow door looked like a wooden scroll about five feet high and was so obviously a framed work of art, one would not easily guess its purpose. The absurd thing was that it opened upon nothing but an alcove, brisk lined and serving no purpose that I could see.

"It hardly seems important enough to be called a secret passage," I agreed, feeling rather silly about my panicky reaction.

In the end, since I didn't want to give the Calders any more trouble than they had at the moment, I left my things in the medieval chamber and went with Bessie to breakfast. I was growing more and more anxious to find out the truth about the Reverend Hawkins' death. Unlike the Calders, as I soon discovered, I wanted some sort of investigation. I wanted to talk to the police, at least to find out the actual cause of his death.

It was a considerable shock, however, to find out that the police were even more anxious to discuss the matter with me. I learned this during breakfast when I discovered everyone was present except Keith. I was dying to know where he might be but I didn't ask. Fortunately for the satisfaction of my curiosity, Bob almost at once wanted to know whether the Reverend

Hawkins' body had been claimed, and if the authorities were done with the matter.

"It still doesn't ring true," he announced, to everyone's discomfort.

"Come now, laddie," his future father-in-law put in with some haste. "A simple heart attack. These tragedies occur all the time. I'm afraid Hawkins never did look very fit. Those thin shanks and that lugubrious face. No. I very much fear it was one of those inevitable things. I only wish it might not have happened here."

I winced at this heartless conclusion, partly because most of us may have been guilty of agreeing with Freddie, at least in secret. Bob muttered something, and Emily reddened and said, "Father! You've no tact at all. If the poor man hadn't climbed those steps, he'd never have had a heart attack."

"The question is, why did he go up there?" Duncan wanted to know. He was frowning, not quite so easygoing and flippant as was his usual habit.

Nor did his wife help matters. "That's what we'd all give a good bit to know. Maybe he'd took a fancy to Nell."

This hardly seemed worth commenting on, although I found it a pretty tasteless remark. And then Bob asked abruptly, "Where has Keith gone? Don't tell me he's working on his precious artifacts!"

Flatly, and with no attempt to play down the news, Freddie said, "Not this morning. They've got him over answering questions in Abbeyvue."

We were all startled. Emily asked anxiously, "Well, do you think they are going to question us all? If so, we had better know ahead of time. I don't know what to say. I didn't see anything. Until Nell called me. Wasn't it a heart attack as everyone said?"

Freddie avoided my eyes. "I believe, as nearly as I could gather, it is Nell they particularly want to interview. Keith made them agree to a more decent hour, but I gather that they base their entire investigation on what they call the 'interesting facts' they would like to learn from her."

"Why me, in particular?"

"It seems—" He examined his Calder-crested butterknife with great intentness. "At all events, the thing occurred in Nell's room, the man went up to her room for some reason none of the rest of us are aware of. She found the body. There are certain drugs missing. These belonged to Nell . . . matters of that sort."

Sending his chair crashing over on its side, Bob got up and exploded, "By God! If that isn't the damnedest nerve! Talk about stupidity! I've heard everything now. We'll just see about this. I'm going over myself and set them straight."

"No, you aren't," I said, though I was intensely grateful for his quick loyalty. "Nothing would give me more satisfaction than to talk with the Abbeyvue Constable."

They all stared at me. It may have been my imagination, but I felt a strong fear in the Calders. And somewhere among them, greed and hatred.

ELEVEN

Immediately after breakfast, I got ready to go ashore, but, of course, the boat was gone and Bob and Duncan, who had both volunteered to take me, went tramping around the island in the intermittent break from the rain squalls, looking for an ancient skiff or something of that sort that could be fitted up with an old engine Duncan guaranteed "might work." There was a high degree of uncertainty in all this, but it had been my experience to let men find out themselves.

"I'm not sure I trust an old skiff and a motor that just might work," I reminded them finally when I could not hold out any longer. Besides, it was momentarily threatening to rain again.

All three of us were on the tiny spit of land at what I thought of as the "front" of the island. We were below the big windows in the lounge which always reminded me of the big observation room on an ocean liner.

"Never mind whether it will work, Sis. We want to get over there as soon as possible and tell that police crowd where to get off. What are they trying to do, railroad you to cover up for their own stupidity?"

"What the hell, old man!" Duncan protested good-naturedly. "This isn't a murder case, you know. What would the Constable be trying to cover up?"

"You know what. The Calders! They run this island like it was on Mars. Not a part of Great Britain at all. And they don't want any crimes investigated, or any island secrets revealed."

I said, "Bob. Don't get carried away," but without seeming to, I noted Duncan Calder's changing expression.

There was the same easy, friendly smile, yet I thought his eyes looked hard, far from smiling. Duncan was more like Keith than he appeared to be at a first or second meeting. He dropped his windbreaker and stooped to pick it up, brushing off the cuff that had trailed into a little rain puddle.

"That's not very friendly, old man." His laugh had in it a nasty strain that seemed a little ominous. Or maybe I was hypersensitive over any reactions of these people. Whatever the Calders felt about me, I didn't want them taking on Bob as well. The wedding had been so near, his happiness and Emy's happiness almost settled. Now, to have this big rift between Calders and Garrisons, over something which might all turn out to be mere accident and coincidence, troubled me even more.

"Look here, Bob . . . Mr. Calder . . . "

"Duncan, Nell. Don't you be forgetting."

"Of course. Duncan. This is silly. We know practically nothing about the vicar's death. And here we are, all quarrelling. We haven't the least idea what we are quarrelling about, either. Wait, at least, until we find out what the police have discovered. It may all be solved simply and quietly and only poor Reverend Hawkins the worse for it." Still, I would have given much to know why the Reverend Hawkins climbed all those steps to see me, if that was why he had gone up there. Could he have gone up to look around when I wasn't there? Highly unlikely. Mrs. Milligan said that everyone thought I'd gone to my room. So the vicar had probably been trying to see me in private.

Something to tell me. And I haven't the faintest notion what that might be.

"But it's all in the family," Duncan agreed at once, resuming that warm, easy facade. He chucked me under the chin. "All in the family, Sis. Damned if I wouldn't marry you myself if I could only—what do you Yanks call it?—*unload* my wife."

This brought back to me vivid memories of Duncan's similar pursuit of the housemaid, Dilys. Of course, he had not made so many fruitful promises to me as to Dilys, but then, she was prettier.

"I wouldn't advise you to unload Bessie," Bob put in, not in his best mood. He glanced over his shoulder, and this made Duncan and me look up. Staring down at us from the center window of the lounge was Bessie Calder. She didn't look at all happy, but then she seldom appeared to be in a good mood. I was uneasy because she had obviously seen Duncan make that stupid gesture of chucking me under the chin, and I wondered if all this was his attempt to cover up the affair with Dilys. In many ways, I found Duncan more mysterious than his quiet, serious half-brother.

When Duncan and I waved to Bessie, she stared at us for an uncomfortable time; then, as if forced to against her inclinations, she waved back. Duncan began to busy himself looking for what I began to suppose was a highly fictitious skiff.

Bob and I walked behind him, carefully making our way to the edge of the stone wall. Below us was foaming, angry water, unpleasantly near. At the same time it began to rain again, and I rushed up the little green triangle of grass toward the walk and the shelter of the great house. I slipped once on the grass, but before Bob or Duncan could reach me, I was walking again. I saw, out of the corner of my eye, the blonde apparition still at the window, and I could have sworn the lips gleamed with a big smile at my accident. The idea rather amused me. It was so human.

"Damn this climate!" Duncan called out, reaching for me, fortunately too late. "If I had my way, and a packet of pound notes, I'd hie me to the South Pacific and bask in sunlight forever."

Bob grinned. "You won't escape the rain just by trading Sea Island for a tropic idyll, Dunc; so don't count on it. May as well get used to these off-and-on storms you have here."

I had reached the narrow walk that ran against the long side of the modern abbey, and was hurrying to avoid the downpour when I saw Keith Calder in the motorboat returning from his visit to Abbeyvue. He waved. I answered and now, in spite of the rain, hurried past the courtyard gate and out to the stone steps and the landing.

"What did you find out? What is the doctor's report? How did he die?"

"One at a time," he warned me, but his smile cancelled out any asperity in his tone. He came up the steps and much to my delight, took my arm as he reached the landing. Had he forgotten all his horrible objections to my money? I devoutly hoped so.

"Do you mind if we don't discuss the matter in front of the others? There are reasons. I want to talk with you later. To discuss what we are to do."

This was a chilling idea. Apparently, as I had suspected, there was more to the Reverend Hawkins' death than mere heart failure. And if there was, I became more and more convinced that I had been the real target. This seemed conceited, egotistical. But logic was with me. Unless we were all very much mistaken about the vicar's private life, he hardly could be said to have an enemy. Certainly not an enemy on Sea Island. Yet, my case was far different. While I had no overt enemies, so many things suggested that the

Calders would be infinitely better off if there were no Elinor Garrison; especially, I thought, as it was well known that Bob was my heir, and Bob was marrying into the Calder family, a family desperately in need of money.

From the moment I arrived at Sea Island, I had sensed a menace . . . or was it only that Bessie Calder's own experience, plus the constant talk of the Calder need for money, warned me?

We had no more than stepped into the courtyard when we found ourselves under siege from everyone in the abbey. It was ludicrous because the rain was coming down hard now, and we were all trying to protect ourselves; yet here were Emily and Freddie Calder and Bessie and, a trifle belatedly, Leander Rumford, looking absent-minded, as if his thoughts were still back there with his psychic vibrations.

Emily rushed up to us first, just as Bob and Duncan, a little slower, approached from the grassy triangle at the tip of the island. Emily's long hair streamed with rain. Her face, totally bare of makeup, looked fresh and lovely. I felt a deep, almost aching regret that this, her wedding day, should be so sad, cancelling out her happiness. It occurred to me as I watched her that perhaps she and Bob could be quietly married ashore in the next day or so.

She grabbed her half-brother by the shoulders, trying to shake him out of his usual calm. It was a funny sight, like a terrier trying to shake a mastiff. As for Keith, his reaction was at once tender and rather fatherly. He was amused and perhaps touched by her youthful enthusiasm, but he wasn't going to be swerved from whatever plans he might have.

"Keith! What happened? Can we go on now, please, as we were? With our plans, I mean . . . make him say yes, Bobbin. Do make him!"

As Bob was busy trying to quiet his talkative fiancee while pulling her away from Keith, Bessie sensibly announced that we were all fools to be drowning here in the rain, and Freddie seconded the motion. But he lingered behind the rest of us as we dashed into the modern half of the abbey, and I heard him trying to pump Keith about the morning's events ashore.

Bessie grumbled to me, "I'll be glad when the business is done, and the poor devil is buried. What a fuss about a simple heart attack! Unless, of course—" She looked back. Keith and the others could not hear her. "—it may turn out to be something quite different. Can you think of any reason why Hawkins should be murdered?"

"Bess, old girl, you're spouting off a bit. Close your clapper!" her husband ordered her inelegantly.

I was surprised when she did so. But then, I had known from the first that whatever his weaknesses, she clearly adored him.

Shortly after, Keith followed me into the lounge where I was nervously looking out at the downpour.

"Elinor, Duncan says they planned to take you ashore, that you and Bob wanted to talk with the authorities."

"I'm afraid Bob was rather upset. He had some notion the police might blame me for—heaven knows what. Letting the vicar die in my room, I suppose."

"Your brother was pretty insistent, but I've persuaded him Emily needs him more than you do."

"Thanks! But if I am to be dragged off to the Tower of London for seducing that poor man up to my room, I may need him more than Emy does."

He smiled. "Not at all. You will have my escort. What about the early part of the afternoon? I'll take you over and you may talk all you like to Constable Maddern. I spent most of the morning with him. A very reasonable man. But you'll find him a good deal puzzled by what happened here last night."

"No more than I am," I said tartly.

I half expected him to add, "Nor I" but he did not. Perhaps he wasn't puzzled. But he did seem suspicious. He reminded me again not to discuss the death with his family, and then was as startled as I, though he tried to hide it, when we saw Freddie across the big room behind us, pouring himself a pre-luncheon sherry. I was surprised that the eavesdropper said nothing, but Keith remarked in a rather unfilial voice,

"Your hand is shaking, Freddie. Had one too many?"

Freddie Calder was up to the occasion, however.

"Never too many, my boy. Truth is, there aren't too many."

All the same, even Keith found it remarkably difficult to fend off questions at lunch, and as for me, I could hardly eat a bite. I was as nervous about meeting the police as if I had killed the Reverend Hawkins myself. I couldn't imagine what motive there would be, but I based all my knowledge of crime and police methods on the examples given on television, especially the late-late shows. From these I was aware that English detectives were always quietest and most polite just before they charged the guilty party with a crime. I had committed no crime. But they could hardly be sure of that.

I did wonder though, as I watched those expressive Calder faces around the table, what secrets they concealed. Bob, too, I thought, was troubled. I caught him glancing rather furtively at the others as I did.

By the time Keith and I started down to the boat during a brief letup in the rain, I also began to suspect Keith's efforts to keep quiet about his interview with the police had only given the Calders a very unpleasant idea about me. They obviously thought I was under suspicion. It didn't raise my own spirits very much. And Bob, with Emy's arm around him, kissed me goodbye as if the whole thing were over and the steel doors clanging shut.

"Keith says I'd only make it worse, Nell. But if anything goes wrong, they make any trouble for you—any at all—you just let me know."

Emy pressed my hand. "Constable Maddern's a sweet one. He'll be nice to you. You must tell him everything." She giggled, trying to make light of the whole business. "All about how Hawkins chased up all those steps to make love to you."

Bob tried to squeeze her waist to silence her, but it was Keith's sharp, "Quiet, brat!" that made her add with a rueful little laugh. "Sorry. See you for cocktails, you two. *We hope*," she added, in a voice of doom that was unmistakable.

We were on our way in no time and I remembered all of Duncan's difficulties with the little boat and its ancient motor. With my sudden and probably vain infatuation for the strong, rock-ribbed man who was my escort now, I felt an enormous pride in him, in his ability to handle any situation. My spirits were raised by this thought, that if he could handle everything else so well, surely he would see that not I but someone in his own family group on the island was responsible for what had happened to the Reverend Hawkins.

But even if he did understand this, could he be generous enough and fair enough to see that I had been the original target? Or was I completely wrong on that score?

We said nothing for a few minutes, and I found myself looking everywhere but at Keith. He, on the other hand, made me exceedingly self-conscious by studying me with an intent look that may have been suspicion, but, perhaps with my woman's intuition, I thought it was warmer than that. Then he said suddenly, "Perhaps you had better spend the night ashore."

"I may not have any choice in the matter. Your family suspects, I'm sure, that I seduced and murdered the vicar. I should be flattered. No one has ever confused me with a *femme fatale* before."

"Ridiculous!"

Incensed, and seeking to change the direction of my nervous thoughts, I teased him, only half joking.

"Well, I like that! What's so ridiculous about me as a *femme fatale*? When I was a child that was my great dream. I hated my name Elinor. Ugh! I wanted to be called Carmelita Gongora."

"Good God!" His hand almost dropped from the motor he was nursing along.

"Oh—" I went on blithely, sweeping off a sudden, vagrant drop of rain, "—I got over that. When I was eight or nine I wanted to be called Ava-Lana. Unfortunately, everybody slurred that to Evalina; so at long last, I surrendered to Elinor Garrison."

He tried to smile, but it was clearly an effort. He reached out with his free hand and squeezed mine hard. The pain of that clasp was oddly sweet to me.

"I'm very glad you aren't Carmelita. Or Ava-Lana. Still, I wish I might change that Elinor Garrison myself. Not that I can do anything about it."

I tried to take this blow lightly. "What a pity! But then, I've had my name so long I'm almost resigned to it."

The big drops of rain began to come down now, sweeping slantwise across the water. I freed my hand, adjusted my ridiculous rain hat with its big, waterproof brim, pulled the collar of my raincoat up around my cheeks, and let it rain.

It gave me a very insecure feeling to see the heavy traffic all around us on the channel, and to realize how very small, how very minute we must appear to those other pilots. But I tried to satisfy myself with the recollection that Keith and the others made this trip all the time and, so far as I knew, had never yet been run over by a tugboat or a scow, or anything larger. By the time we reached the little jetty at Abbeyvue, I was forming whole sentences of complaint about the death of the Reverend Hawkins, about the things that had happened since, and the idea of my being blamed.

"Already to brave the fates?" Keith asked me as he lifted me out of the boat. I could have climbed myself, but was by no means averse to this method of setting foot on the stone quay.

I shook off the raindrops, laughed to soothe him and especially myself, and said: "Lead on, General!" I added a little less confidently, "I hope you will act as my solicitor, just in case they have me headed for Wormwood Scrubs . . . that is your prison; isn't it?"

"We do have more than one. At any rate, you may count on me, although I have never been accused of having a silver tongue. Quite the contrary." He took my arm and we started up that ghastly, cobbled street which was almost vertical. "You aren't afraid; are you? Maddern is a very decent chap. You may tell him in confidence anything you know or suspect about the business in that room."

I looked at him uneasily. "But I don't really know anything about it. I only—nothing."

"You suspect. Do you suspect anything definite?"

"I was meant to be the real victim." I blurted it out and was instantly sorry. It did not make me feel very much more self-assured to find that Keith did not deny this. The only good thing about his attitude was that he must really know the danger, always assuming there was a danger to me, now that the poor vicar had died in my place.

"I wasn't sure that you knew the implications. You

had better stay ashore tonight. I can't let you go back there thinking that."

"Then you think so too."

He looked away, as if he found the picturesque little cottages along the street exceedingly interesting. "I don't know. But I am convinced that the vicar was not meant to die. And he did die of those capsules that belonged to you. I suppose it is even vaguely possible that he took them for some obscure reason and—no! It's too fantastic. But there were grains of those sleeping powders in the glass I gave them when they took Hawkins away. I spent almost the entire morning discussing this other thing—that the wrong victim died—with Constable Maddern. It wasn't very pleasant, as you can imagine. But then," he looked down at me. His voice softened. "It is even more unpleasant to think it might have been you."

"I couldn't agree with you more."

We agreed, while not saying so aloud, that we had better not pursue this subject without having more proof. I could see how the idea of murder in his own family would be a frightful thought for Keith to face. I admired him more than ever for his long view of the event. It must be terribly difficult for him to be objective. And anyway, an emotional part of my mind clung to the hope that there was another explanation for the death of the vicar.

"Here we are."

I looked over at the delightful little house half-way up the hill. It might have been Ye Olde Tea Shoppe except that the front windows on either side of the door were not bays, and there was no name advertised. Not even the police department, or whatever the British equivalent was, seemed to be announced. I suppose I must have looked surprised because Keith explained as we crossed the heavy, deeply rounded cobblestones, "There is another entrance, a trifle more official, on the next street. But I thought it better to attract less attention this way."

"Thank you. It's much better." But in spite of his good intentions, my raincoat and bright rain hat had already earned me some interested stares, but I found this interest far less frightening than the easy friendship of the Calders, one of whom might be trying to murder me. Keith hadn't quite touched the latch of the door when it opened ominously inward. Keith put an arm around my waist, offering both physical and moral support, and we went in.

There was no hall. We found ourselves in a small, almost Victorian, quaint parlor with a clutter of furniture and wallpaper. The man who had opened the door looked rather like a sergeant in a Hollywood version of Gallant Britain at War. He was no taller than I, and had a distinctly trustworthy manner. He would have been perfectly cast as the little chap who made jokes to lighten the company's tension, and might very possibly fall on the live bomb, blowing himself up to save the regiment. I would have liked him in a movie, but in real life his hazel eyes seemed to X-ray me even as he smiled and greeted both of us. Keith introduced us. The heroic little sergeant turned out to be Constable Maddern, out of uniform.

"Do sit down, Ma'am. Some tea, would you say? You Yanks—Americans—seem to expect it, somehow."

I refused with a nervous smile, but Keith countermanded my refusal and before I knew it I was drinking some very strong tea, served by a tall, lanky, serious-faced man, and relating my part in last night's events while those X-ray hazel eyes kept note of my every expression, every inflection, never missing a thing.

"And you'd never met him before, this Reverend Hawkins? Never been given any indication that he had something to say to you in private? A confidential message, in fact?"

"I had no idea at all. I hardly noticed him, and he certainly took no interest in me. Did you see anything in his manner, Keith, that might have suggested he wanted to tell me some secret?"

"Nothing whatever. But I do believe—"

"Not just now, Mr. Calder. Later, if you don't mind."

Keith glanced at me. "If you feel more comfortable now, I think you and Maddern will hit it off very well without me. Call me when you've done with your talk." I must have looked my dismay and uneasiness because Keith got up to go, stopped, touched my cheek gently with his forefinger and added, "Tell him all you suspect. Don't spare us, any of us. Do you understand what I am saying, Elinor?"

I caught Constable Maddern's calm, direct gaze, and shivered. "I—I think so. I'll tell you all I know about it, but I'm afraid there is nothing definite. Nothing concrete enough to work on."

"Possibly," Maddern agreed in that dangerously friendly and unprepossessing voice. "But you might just send your thoughts back, so to speak, and let us judge it in the light of what we all know from other sources."

When Keith had gone into the next room and closed the door with a firm click of the latch, I was amazed to find myself much freer, less anxious to weigh every word.

"I know mere suspicion is worthless as evidence," I began tentatively.

Maddern made a little motion like brushing away flies.

"Quite so. But your suspicions, without your knowing it, may lead our investigation on the right path, so to speak. I am free to tell you that Mr. Keith Calder brought an item or two to our attention, conclusively proving that the Reverend Hawkins drank from a glass of water in your room and died as a result."

"My water glass. I always have a water glass ready in case I should be thirsty in the night. I suppose a carafe would be more sensible, but it's an old habit."

"Who places that water glass for you at Sea Abbey?"

"Dilys, I imagine. Or possibly Mrs. Milligan."

"Dilys is the upper servant. A maid? Housekeeper?"

"A maid. So the vicar died of those sleeping pills of mine. I suspected it when I found they had disappeared."

"When was that? Did anyone know about them?"

"I suppose so. I left one out the previous night but didn't take it. Anyone could have seen it. I discovered the loss shortly after I found the vicar's body."

Before I knew it, he had the whole story of my suspicions, including the fact that I believed I was the intended victim.

"I may tell you, Miss Garrison, that Mr. Keith Calder shares this suspicion. His family is hard pressed for money . . . is that the motive, to your mind?"

"Yes. My brother is marrying the Calder girl, and if anything happened to me, he would be my heir."

Maddern coughed. "May I point out a slight difficulty? Mr. Calder seems to think his father has matrimonial designs on you. Wouldn't that be an easier way of obtaining your fortune?" He seemed to find it embarrassing to mention my money, but I believed by this time that it was at the root of the attempt to kill me . . . if, of course, I was the intended victim.

"And with these little clues, we have no proof."

"In a case like this," I reminded him, "I'd have to sit around and wait for the murderer to strike again, to give us proof. Not a very nice prospect."

"Of course," he agreed, almost too quickly. "It is impossible. A pity, though. Still, as you remind me, we must take them all as suspects. Frederic and Duncan and Keith and the ladies . . ."

"Not Keith!"

He shrugged. "Until we know more, we cannot remove anyone from our little list."

"Yes, but it can't be Keith. Why, he gave you what evidence there was."

"Very true. If only we could decoy this would-be murderer to reveal himself! But I'm afraid we cannot rely solely on our friend Keith. I still maintain he is, theoretically, suspect."

About this time I had a very strong suspicion myself. Maddern wanted me to return to the island. He doubtless hoped the person who emptied the powder into that glass would try again. It wasn't a very cheerful idea and I became completely blank, not understanding the slightest hint.

It was not until our interview was over that I began to wonder if all his questioning of me was a put-on. He might even suspect me of the crime. I was asked to repeat all my suspicions, every shred of knowledge I could dredge up while a thin, middle-aged woman with bright eyes and prominent teeth took dictation directly on her typewriter.

Constable Maddern was his polite self as Keith and I left. "Well, well, good afternoon to you both. I won't say goodbye. In all probability we will be seeing each other again soon. Perhaps tomorrow."

"He thinks I did it," I said coldly when we were beyond the Constable's hearing.

"On the contrary. I believe he suspects me. When he isn't busy suspecting the rest of the family. The investigation is going to be turned over to more sophisticated procedures from Bristol as soon as the men arrive, but I doubt if they are more skillful than Maddern. Meanwhile, I'll bring over your things. You will spend the night in the village. Tomorrow you should be on your way to London. A deposition ought to satisfy Maddern."

I almost said yes. But I knew if I went off to London, assuming Maddern would let me leave, I would very likely never see Keith again. Apparently he thought so, too. We looked at each other for a long moment, ignoring the rain.

"If I go," I reminded him, "we will always be wondering. You and I may even be wondering about each other."

"What else is possible? We can't have you risking further violence just to prove it can happen. Besides, Maddern may learn something tonight."

"Tonight!"

"Yes. From a hint or two I gathered that he will be coming over tonight on some pretext. Probably so he can observe us all in our . . . natural habitat."

I jumped at this chance to keep from leaving and still avoid being murdered, or at any rate, scared to death.

"But then, it would be quite safe for me to remain on the island another day or two. And if I am there it will certainly make it easier for Bob and Emy. If I ran away like a coward, everything would be awkward for them." I was ashamed of my own hypocrisy over using the poor lovers as my excuse when my real urge was to be near Keith, but I could not tell him that.

"I don't like it." But I knew he recognized the truth of what I said.

I pretended high spirits about the whole thing. "You don't seem very cheerful at the prospect of another evening in my company."

"Nell! Don't be funny when your life may be at

stake!" I thought he was going to shake me, but he restrained himself, though he did shake a few raindrops off my sleeves.

I laughed at his anger, his tension. "If you fail me, I can always get Freddie to show me his wine cellar again."

His anger crumbled to a reluctant laugh and instead of shaking me, he hugged me. We were in the middle of the street and so many people saw us I felt as if we were on Cinemascope. So did he, I think, but he still kept his arm around me as we walked down to the little quay at the foot of the hill.

By the time we got into the boat, the rain had turned into a torrent, and wind squalls were lashing it against us. I felt lucky to be Keith's company. I knew that he, if anyone, could handle the boat in these crowded waters, besieged on every side by tankers, barges and innumerable weird, tooting objects that darted out of the gray mist like ghostly apparitions.

Nevertheless, I was intensely glad to see the familiar landing and the steps of Sea Abbey a short time later, and to know that Bob and Emy and Duncan were there anxiously waiting for our safe arrival. I could hardly make out anything beyond their figures, however. The rain was a heavy curtain, almost brown with pigment and smog from the surrounding industrial areas along the busy shorelines.

Between Bob's hand and Duncan's, I was quickly drawn up out of the boat, but as I walked up the steps to the landing my way was blocked by smiling, pink-faced little Leander Rumford.

"You see. You were all wrong about the lady. She came back in spite of everything. You aren't afraid of my astral phenomena; are you, dear lady?"

"Stow it!" Duncan called to him, grinning, but rather troubled.

Leander was unsquelched. "Miss Nell! You were wise to return. This is a perfect night for some manifestations. I think I can promise you a merry time."

TWELVE

During cocktails, Emily drinking what Bob insisted must be a "thin" gin-and-tonic, repeatedly asked what had happened to Keith and me, and if anyone was about to be "taken in charge." She shivered with childish delight.

"Taken in charge! What a thrilling sound that is! And standing trial in the Old Bailey, and having everyone fascinated about whether you are guilty or not! It's too marvelous. Don't you think so, Bobbin?"

We were all laughing except Bob and Bessie Calder. Bob insisted, "Not a bit marvelous if you were the one standing trial."

Bessie sat gloomily behind Duncan, tossing off her father-in-law's martinis with one hand while the other curled up the straggling, coppery ends of her husband's hair. Staring into her empty glass she murmured sourly, "For all we know, the whole lot of us will be behind the bars before this business is settled." Everyone looked up self-consciously, and she added, "The whole rotten thing would be over by now if we only knew what the bloody hell old Hawkins was wanting in Nell's room."

No one said anything. We were all shaken by the ugly truths in Bessie's words. Then Leander Rumford startled us all. He had been in the hallway entrance to the lounge, forgotten by all of us, until he reminded us smugly, "It may be he wished to bring her a message. A warning."

Duncan burst out, "Must you blather like that? Father, I think we've done our share for the Psychic Association. I move we close shop and make an end of all these damned ghosts and other quirks."

Keith, beside me, called across the room: "Patience, old boy!" But Leander's protests were pitiful enough to draw tears, and a small, ultra-polite argument began between him and Freddie Calder. Bessie came over to the sideboard, poured herself a straight gin, but did not drink it all. She stopped to hear the argument, especially her husband's part.

Keith glanced at me with his rare, gentle smile. "I'm glad you came back." Then, as if afraid of sentimentality, he remarked in a low tone, "But I must admit, we will all be relieved when Leander departs with his ectoplasm, his apparitions and his extraordinary imagination."

"I don't understand why he is here at all when neither you nor Duncan want him."

"Freddie is the owner of Sea Island," he reminded me. "And I have a sneaking notion Rumford's foundation has been paying Freddie a tidy little fee, along with his expenses."

That explained a good deal. But it didn't make things any easier for the rest of us. The ill-feeling was still present among us all during dinner, but although much of it was manifest toward Leander Rumford, he kept his cool, never losing his temper or his fat smile.

I had been wondering during the evening where I would sleep that night. This and the intermittent quarrels among the Calders occupied me so that I didn't notice Keith's growing uneasiness until Mr. Rumford suggested escorting me to my room, presumably that gigantic medieval chamber he had loaned to me last night.

"Maybe I had better go to my room," I said to Keith. "It's getting late and so far, we've accomplished nothing."

"Looks as though Maddern won't get here tonight. I think I'll call him when I can do so without the entire house listening in."

"Don't call on my account. I won't drink water tonight, except from the tap. And I'll keep the door—" Not locked. I couldn't lock either of the rooms assigned to me. But I could barricade them. And I would!

He took my hands in his, under the bright, interested gaze of Leander Rumford. "I'll drop by later, to see how you are doing." He said this rather loudly, which was most unlike him. But I understood. He was warning the family, making it clear that he might be around, in case anyone tried anything. At least, I told myself, that must be his intention!

For a group that had been in an extraordinarily, almost unnaturally convivial mood that evening, the Calders all became subdued with suspicious haste when bedtime came. I suspected they were all as nervous as I was. All but one of them. Bob was going to take Emy to her room, and offered to go as far as the old abbey building with Leander and me. We passed Bessie and Duncan, outside their suite, quarrelling as usual, but Duncan stopped abruptly as we came by. We said good night to the pair and when we were just stepping out into the courtyard, we heard Bessie's shrewish voice:

"You stay out of my bed tonight, and you'll stay out for good and all, my lad! No running around after servants and pretty lady guests. You hear me!"

"You could hear her in London!" Emy whispered, giggling on a note of hysteria. Bob pulled her close to him lovingly and Mr. Rumford nudged me.

"First love. Enchanting. Like seeing two souls in Elysium."

"Let's hope these two remain alive and out of Elysium for a while," I reminded him more sharply than I meant to. It wasn't this little fellow's fault that he was gullible and believed in his preposterous ghosts.

"I hope the electric system remains on duty, at least for tonight," I said as we crossed the courtyard.

Either Emily found my remark unexpectedly funny, or she still had a carryover from her hysteria.

"But you are so silly, Nell! There was no electric trouble in our part of the abbey. Our part of the abbey had its troubles, but they weren't the absence of electricity."

"Don't be flip, Sweetheart!"

It was plain to me that Bob had his work cut out for him in marrying this likable, spontaneous youngster, but being in a romantic mood myself, I wished them well and felt that if this ghastly murder business could be solved without hurting Emy too much, she and Bob probably would be as likely to have a happy marriage as most couples.

They said good night to me at the beginning of the long flight of steps leading to the upper level, and Mr. Rumford took me around the corner to that incredible museum piece which he very obligingly surrendered to me for another night. I protested sincerely. Heaven knows I was sincere in claiming that I didn't want to rob him of his sleeping quarters, especially *these* quarters!

But Dilys, pushing her way out of the room at that minute, seemed to put the final touches to Leander Rumford's offer.

"It's all arranged, Miss. Your property has been moved down here. Mr. Freddie Calder's order. You'll be more comfortable, he said."

"I see. Thank you. Oh—Dilys, did you leave a glass of water beside the bed?"

"Not beside it, Ma'am. There's no night stand. But it's all fresh-drawn, the full carafe of water. On one of those funny things Mr. Keith calls cabarets."

"Tabarets, my dear," Leander corrected her gently. "I'll leave you now, Miss Nell—if I may call you Nell."

"But where are you sleeping, Mr. Rumford?"

He clutched my arm to punctuate what was clearly a passionate enthusiasm. His small, round eyes were oddly appealing, like eyes freshly washed.

"You can't imagine! I dreamed of a visitation last night. It must have been the Reverend Hawkins. It happened so shortly after he passed over into the great . . ."

"Beyond?"

"Er—yes. We don't put it quite that way. You see, they are happy!"

"Then why do they want to come back?"

"There are excellent reasons. Most excellent. Believe me. I am not at liberty to divulge them quite yet, but give me a trifling of time, and it shall be done."

"If you say so. But it's so uncomfortable in that awful place where you are to sleep."

There was no convincing him; so we said good night and he went his way, along that uneven, tunnel-like passage into the grim and terrible heart of this island. Dilys would have left me, rather hurriedly, I thought, but I called to her.

"Dilys, who usually puts the water glass by my bed?"

I may have been wrong but I could almost have sworn she was merely puzzled, not the least nervous or worried, or sly about answering me directly.

"Me, Miss. It was me. If you'd like hot cocoa, it could be arranged. Mrs. Milligan always has it. Kind of a nightcap, as Mr. Bobbin calls it. Mrs. Milligan told me to leave the water for you, but she said if you was to make a preference for cocoa, we was to leave that."

"No, thank you. And no one else touched the water either last night or tonight?"

"Nobody. Leastways, I don't see who. I hope it wasn't bitter, Miss. The chemicals, they make it taste awful sometimes."

There was obviously nothing more to be gotten from Dilys. I thanked her again, agreed that it must be the chemicals, and she went out. I heard her crossing the courtyard a minute later.

I was alone.

I went into that absurd, yet grand medieval chamber, and tried to bring the door shut behind me. The screeching of that door was enough to make my teeth ache. At any rate, it would require just as much effort, as much noise for someone to get in to me. I did the best I could. I pulled it almost shut. I looked around, still wondering, half suspecting there might be something hanging around here that belonged to Leander Rumford. I looked in the closet. My clothes were there. Nothing else had been placed there since last night.

Eventually, having circled the room and found absolutely nothing, not even behind the bed curtains, I peeked into the bathroom. By this time I was beginning to feel perfectly ridiculous. I got out my night clothes, ran a bath whose water was lukewarm and, unfortunately, not too clean-looking. I briskly rubbed myself down with a very rough terry cloth robe. Having opened the window drape to give me some light, I snapped off the electric light overhead, and made a bee-line for the steps to the huge bed.

Someone, probably Dilys, had put a hot water bottle in my bed, which startled me a little, but as the night was cold and damp, the bottle proved to have been an inspiration. I covered myself up, gradually grew drowsy and warm, and went off to sleep.

I was to discover later that Keith had stealthily looked in on me through the door, which remained open about two inches, and being satisfied that I was all right, he went his way.

At somewhere close to two o'clock all this peace, warmth and quiet was shattered, for me at least, by several half-strangled cries. Or sobs. It was hard to tell, but they roused me to consciousness, besides frightening me into an almost frozen state.

"Who—who is it?" I shouted. "Where are you?"

I can't think why I said that. Anyone making the noise I had heard was certainly in no condition to identify himself. As there were no other sounds for a minute or two, I began to think over what I had heard, and remembering last night, became disgusted with myself; since I had obviously been awakened by my own screams, due to some nightmare or other. Hadn't Keith heard me and come running last night?

I settled back, plumped up the pillows, and tried to return to sleep, at the same time wondering what nightmare had obsessed me so much I awoke screaming two nights in a row. No, I thought. That can't have happened. Surely, I was fully awakened when I heard that last shriek of unbelieving horror.

In spite of these doubts, I almost convinced myself that it had all been my doing, the screams and the nightmares. The unfamiliar noises I heard. Of course they were unfamiliar! I had never slept in such a place before last night.

But they certainly were odd sounds. Try as I would to cover my ears and sink back into the soft comfort of the bed, I kept hearing noises that had nothing to do with any nightmare of mine. Probably the wind made those weird, moaning sounds. I lay there tossing and turning, counting horns as they tooted from boats of varying sizes in the channel surrounding the island.

The moan of the wind was unnerving. I punched a pillow angrily. That devilish moan! Like a man so completely terrified, he had become an infant again, in a very agony of fear.

"It's too ridiculous! The door of this room should be closed. No wonder I keep hearing the moan of the wind and other absurd noises."

I worked myself up into such a rage, I got out of bed, stepped into my slippers and fumbled around in the cold air for the light switch. The dim light came on, blinding me momentarily. I fumbled through the wardrobe for a warm cloth coat, shrugged into it and tied the belt in a big, clumsy knot. Then I stood by the great door, peeking out through the two inches that exposed the passage, and feeling idiotic. There was not a thing out there that shouldn't be found in any normal, everyday medieval passage leading to a vault and altar reputedly haunted!

Like Emy a few hours ago, I had a strong desire to laugh hysterically. But of course, that might have drowned out the sound of the moaning in the church interior where Leander Rumford was sleeping. I listened. That wasn't the wind. It was a human being suffering a great emotional trauma. I pushed at the door, pushed hard. The squeaking began, changing to a screech as metal scraped over the uneven stones of the passage. I finally got the door open enough to squeeze through.

I had already called out earlier; so I felt that I could hardly cause more commotion if I called out now.

"Mr. Rumford? Are you all right?"

My voice came back to me in bits and pieces, eery and wavering. Surely, I hadn't sounded so frightened! What a coward I was becoming lately, afraid to go into a church itself to help a man who seemed to be in the last stage of terror!

On the other hand, remembering the poisoned water last night, I decided not to dash off along the passage to that hideous altar without some kind of weapon. From the light in my room which cut dimly across the passage, I made out a brick or two on the floor in a far corner of the passage, but nothing I could use as a weapon. I moved away from the great medieval chamber under the steps, sure now that the sounds I heard were genuine moans from somewhere along the church nave. Just beyond the stone steps leading to the upper level, I found a castaway poker. I've no idea what it was doing there, probably used long ago to stoke a rousing blaze in one of the ancient fireplaces.

Furious, in order to cover my fears, I went striding along the tunnel toward the altar where either poor, believing Mr. Rumford or some unexpected visitor was groaning and muttering. I had a death grip on the old poker. I almost fell when I reached the church vestibule just outside the nave where Leander Rumford presumably had been sleeping. As Freddie reminded me two evenings ago, I had to watch my step here where, at one time or other, repairs had been started and left half-completed. I caught myself just in time, stepped into the high-beamed church interior, which was lighted eerily by some sort of psychedelic lamp on the altar. This affair revolved with a myriad of colors and seemed to bring out the little brightness remaining in the stained glass windows of the north wall.

"Mr. Rumford? Are you all right?"

There was a writhing, moaning bundle beneath the altar. Horrified to discover that this was our fearless, smiling Leander Rumford, I knelt beside him, setting the poker down.

"Here . . . wake up! What happened? Look at me. You're perfectly all right. Come now, Leander, control yourself."

"Standing there . . . just—staring—"

"Who? There is no one here. Nobody but you and me." I looked around though, wondering, uneasy. It was terribly cold. There was a simple explanation for that, however. This was the middle of the night, after all, and the church was built into the rocky core of the island.

"Shall I get you some water?"

"No! Don't leave me. Don't—oh, my God! It was standing there behind the altar."

"What was? You mean someone tried to harm you?"

"Not someone. Some *thing*. It was risen from the dead. A monk."

I was bewildered. I didn't believe in the dead coming back. But Mr. Rumford did. And here he was, making this terrible fuss because he thought the thing he prayed for had come true.

"You are here to make these very discoveries, Mr. Rumford. You wanted the dead to come back. I'll admit that the sight of a sixteenth century monk in this horrible tomb would send me into the jitters, but I don't understand your attitude at all."

"It was—it was so real. Not the way I thought it would be. Why . . ." His round, innocent eyes stared up at me pitifully. ". . . the *thing* wasn't friendly. It did not emerge from the mist. It simply was there, staring down at me from behind the altar. It was—livid."

I looked around again. I might be entirely convinced that the dead did not come back, but there was a prickle of fear along my spine, all the same.

"Come, now. We're going to get out of here.

You're cold. That is all. You're cold and you are imagining things. Here. Lean on me."

I thought I had him convinced, but as I was getting him to his stocking feet, he pointed a shaking hand at the altar behind me, his face strange, multi-colored in the lamplight.

"There—again! Merciful God! Don't let it touch me. I beg you. Don't—"

I had my arm under his shoulders and I very nearly dropped him as I looked back.

There was a monk staring at me. The eyes were sunk deep in the shadowing cowl of his robe.

THIRTEEN

"I don't believe it. *I don't believe it!*"

I blinked and looked again. But it was there. The hideous, unmoving, cowled head, the eyes deep within. And at last I recovered my senses enough to scream. I must have electrified poor Mr. Rumford, who scrambled to his feet, still pointing a shaking hand in my direction, or rather, behind me. He tried to run away, along the sunken stones that once marked the main aisle of the church, but he stumbled badly.

Something glistened above my head, between the cowled head and my own. I screamed again, but this time I recognized the threat. The weapon over my head was the age-dulled metal crucifix that had threatened me once before. Idiot that I was, I had dropped the poker to raise Leander Rumford! But I had dropped it very near, almost underfoot. I ducked that swinging blow, feeling behind me for the poker.

One thing was belatedly clear to me, frightened as I might be at this sinister apparition. Our sixteenth century monk was very real. No ghostly apparition would float around waving corporeal weapons. The crucifix struck the altar a loud, ringing blow, and just missed my face. I cried out again, backing down, and prayed my groping fingers would find the poker.

Somewhere behind me beyond the church entrance, I heard running feet and I cried out again. At the

same time the lamp was overturned and all those terrifying, whirling little psychedelic lights Leander had
been using for his experiments disappeared. We were
in darkness. But only briefly. The running footsteps
arrived along with the bright but constricted glow of
a flashlight. I was expecting Keith but it was Duncan
who arrived with the flashlight. His face looked pale
and drawn, and the light shook in his hand.

"What's going on here? What has happened?"

"It is in here. The thing—the one who murdered the
vicar, he's here!"

Duncan turned the flashlight in various directions,
showing up the time-stained walls with their dark
water streaks, the heavy, shadowed beams overhead
probably alive with spiders and other fellows of the
dark, and the sad loveliness of the stained glass window, patched and boarded up.

"Gone now, old dear! You certain it was someone
human? Not one of Leander's—um—thing-gummies?"

Leander Rumford scrambled back to Duncan,
clutching at Duncan's long leg to help himself to his
feet.

"Yes, yes! It was one of the dead come back. But so
malignant. He came through the veil of death, but
only to hurt."

I had been so scared I now felt furious at having,
for a few seconds, been taken in by that so-called apparition. "Don't be silly! This was one of us. Somebody on Sea Island. Somebody who tried to kill us."

"Where?"

I pointed back at the altar and almost before Leander and I could duck out of the way, Duncan
stretched one long arm between us and began to hammer at what remained of the altarpiece. Failing to do
anything but raise dust, he went around behind the altar, pursued by Leander's anxious voice.

"It came out of the wall there. Or so it seemed."

Duncan began to bang at the wall, along the center of the heavy stone blocks. He was still vainly hammering away when Keith Calder's welcome voice called to us from the archway of the entrance. Like his brother, he was fully dressed. Had they been up all night?

"What is it? What the devil are you doing, Duncan?"

"They say it came from this wall. Some apparition or other."

"It was not an apparition. It was a real, flesh-and-blood human being," I insisted, but Duncan was making so much noise, he could not hear me.

Keith set his own flashlight on the altar to illuminate their work, and going back to the far wall where his father kept his pet wine cellar, surprised me by picking up a crowbar. He brought this over beside Duncan and began to pry out the crumbling, death-gray substance that had been used to seal in the stones. In no time, the great stones began to loosen like rotting teeth. While I stood there, appalled at this act which seemed to me almost like sacrilege, Keith cried, "It's coming. Watch it!"

Both men leaped out of the way as a wall of stones five feet high fell forward to the floor, with a crash that raised quantities of gritty dust. I covered my face, coughing, and only opened my eyes to hear Leander Rumford beside me murmur,

"Oh, My God! My God!"

"We should have guessed before this," Duncan said quietly. "This wall was replaced in the last couple of hundred years. Look at the mortar."

For a minute I could not see what they were talking about. When I finally moved forward, however, I was able to make out dimly the horror they had found sealed in the narrow recess behind that wall. It was the skeletal remains of a human being, standing there with bits of rotted cloth between the remaining teeth, and rags still hanging from various bones. What we saw was one of those wretched convicts gagged and sealed in the walls of Sea Abbey by that eighteenth century Duncan Calder, so that a rapid, uninterested search by the London government would not reveal that he had failed to deliver his shipload of convicts Down Under to Botany Bay. This poor devil had served his purpose like the others, no doubt, and having helped in the work of reconstruction at Sea Abbey, had been in the way at the wrong time during an inspection. This was the result. How many others were likewise hidden in the walls, doomed to suffer this monstrous death?

I think we were all equally shocked, even though the fact itself had been accepted by the family and by historians for years. But it was Leander Rumford who compounded the horror.

"That explains it; don't you see?" he cried. "The creature we saw was the avenging spirit of that convict sealed alive, to die so hideously. He thought I was a Calder. So he threatened me."

Keith looked at me. In his quiet, reassuring way he asked, "What did you really see, Elinor?"

"Not a phantom," I said firmly. "I am sure of that."

I explained as briefly as possible about the night's events and what I had witnessed.

"Don't you see, Keith, it couldn't have been a—a spirit. A ghost. This was real. See where the crucifix fell. It came down with some force. Human force. Apparitions don't need weapons of that size."

"Darling, I know it. You need not convince me. But what did he—or she—look like? Do you remember details? Anything at all?"

I tried to think, but nothing occurred to me. I looked quickly around the great, grim interior. It was obvious that whoever had frightened us escaped some time during the minute or two that Mr. Rumford's lamp had been broken and plunged us into darkness.

Keith reached for me, asking if I was all right.

"Yes. I just want to get out of here." I lowered my voice. "I think Mr. Rumford may need something to calm him. He's had a terrible shock."

He smiled. "And you? You are perfectly fit. No shocks?"

"That's because I am mad."

"Mad!"

"Angry. Furious. A member of your loving family scared him and tried to kill me. So, you see, I haven't room to be frightened." It was a demonstrable lie. He had only to touch me, as he did now, to see how I was shaking. But I was angry, all the same.

With his arm around me protectively, Keith said, "Duncan, there is nothing we can do at this hour. The main thing is to take care of Elinor and Leander. We can get back to this in the morning." Duncan and Leander Rumford, the latter in great confusion, unable to walk, were arguing about the thing in the wall, and Keith whispered to me, "I expect Maddern any minute. I was on my way to the landing when I heard the commotion in here."

"Thank heaven!" I said, but I wasn't altogether sure that Constable Maddern, no matter how skillful, could discover which of the Calders was behind all this. Only an insider could know, I thought.

Duncan sighed. "I daresay it will all have crumbled to dust by morning." But to my surprise he lifted the psychic researcher into his arms with impressive ease. He gave an abrupt, coarse laugh and indicated the skeleton with his head. "That one won't walk away." He started up the aisle, looked around with his shivering burden. "Where is a safe place for him?"

"Please . . . my room. Quite safe," the little man murmured plaintively.

Keith said, "Impossible. Miss Garrison has that room tonight."

But in my anger I had an idea. I asked the Calders to give that medieval chamber back to Mr. Rumford. "I'm going to sleep in the room on the upper level. It's only a few hours until daylight anyway."

"No! I forbid it."

"Keith, I have an idea. Come with me."

He asked no questions. Perhaps he guessed. We went ahead of Duncan and his squirming burden and as we hurried along Keith flashed his light into corners, before us, and even overhead, but I think we both knew that whoever had masqueraded as the monk was not hanging around waiting for applause. Unless it had been Duncan Calder.

Keith pushed open the heavy door of that sleeping chamber so that his brother could get in with Leander Rumford. Then, under my direction, he took a handful of my clothes from the wardrobe and, slightly embarrassed, took out lingerie, also under my instructions. Then we started up the worn and sloping steps. Our feet echoed as if a whole regiment went before us up those steps.

"What is this all about?" he asked abruptly.

I was all innocence. I was sick and tired of all these near-misses and I meant to find out, to trap, if possible, the murderous creature in back of the evils at Sea Island. I didn't want to tell Keith about my plan. I knew he would refuse to cooperate. On the other hand, I had a perfectly legitimate reason for protecting myself.

"I want to ask you a great favor."

He started to say something, smiled wryly, and said then, "I had better learn what it is before I agree."

"I would like you to get me a gun. A handgun."

He sighed. "I was afraid of something like that.

Don't trouble to give me your reasons. They are sure to be impossible."

"Not to me. They make perfect sense. I believe more than ever, since that business in the church tonight, that I am the target of this murderer. Or murderess. You aren't going to find out who it is by police methods. You are going to have to do just as I do. Wait for the next move against me."

"Nell! Are you out of your mind?"

"Perfectly sane. I am not going to wander into dark attics or even slippery sewers to be ambushed. But I am going to prepare myself and then pretend I haven't, and try and entice whoever it is to move against me."

"I refuse. Categorically."

"You haven't anything to say about it. Except to get me a gun. A pistol. A revolver. Whatever I can handle easily."

We argued in low voices until we reached the upper level. By that time I suppose he must have seen that I had a valid point and yielded, partially.

"If you will lock yourself into that room—"

"There is a remarkably poor lock."

"Put something in front of the door then. It will only be a few minutes, until I return with Maddern."

"And Constable Maddern hides under my bed until whoever it is makes an appearance."

"Something like that. Yes."

I couldn't really see anything wrong with the idea, providing it was done in strictest secrecy. "But if the murderer sees Maddern, or guesses at all that he is in the room with me, then it's all off."

"Trust Maddern and me for that. I am only worried about leaving you alone now for five minutes. You must promise me not to let anyone in until I return."

"Secret passwords and all that?"

Reluctantly, he grinned. "I'll make myself known. But promise me—" He opened the door for me and stepped into the room with me, looking around. Then he went over to the tiny balcony. I reminded him not to let himself be seen, but he got a pretty accurate view of the balcony from the French door, and came back. "All right. Promise not to open to anyone at all, except to me, and to Maddern. Agreed?"

"Heartily. It may surprise you to know, I've no anxiety to get myself killed."

He kissed me, a comradely, fun kiss, then his lips moved from my forehead to my lips, and for a long, delicious moment, we kissed. And I thought, when we parted, that I had told the truth. I was very anxious not to die. There might be too much ahead. I wasn't going to let Keith talk himself out of his love for me. At the door, as I closed it, I had to promise him again. Then I stuck a chair under the knob, and piled a hassock on top of the chair.

I turned around and studied the cozy little room with its pink glow from the lamp Keith had snapped on. "All right," I thought, "I might as well begin to play the guinea pig." I kept my courage by the knowledge that if I was very careful, I could stop this terror once and for all. It was by physical action that I used that nervous energy and pretended not to notice my own inner panic.

I went to the French door, opened it and went out, moving carefully, onto the tiny balcony, deliberately letting myself be seen by the person responsible for these attempted crimes. While I was out there, I thought of Emily, who had access to my room from the same balcony. Moving with great care, I edged my way around the corner to her door and peered in. The thick fog had risen a trifle and somewhere far above us, dawn was trying to peer through that smoggy barrier. I made out the form of Emily Calder in a tumbled heap among the bedcovers.

Since there hardly seemed any danger from that quarter, I moved cautiously back to my room. I took off my coat, keeping on the peignoir and gown, hoping to look more natural for that mysterious and detestable creature who had set out to kill me and was willing to kill anyone else in the way. I pulled the covers back, preparatory to settling down in bed as if expecting no trouble, but then I decided I needed a weapon, just in case Keith and Maddern did not return in the next few minutes.

A hand rattled the door knob in the hall. I swung around, ice-cold, all my bones stiff with fear. "A fine way to behave!" I told myself furiously. "Snap out of it!" I wanted to call out, to ask who was there, because if it was Keith, he would certainly tell me so. But I stood there wavering uncertainly between speaking out and simply pretending I was asleep so that whoever it was would try to break in, and maybe be tricked into confessing his guilt.

The rattling of the door knob was sharp now, and angry. Or panicked? And then a voice:

"Nell! Let me in."

For an instant I thought it was Keith. I almost spoke out in answer.

"I must talk to you, old girl. Nell, I know you're there. Open up!"

That ancient, British slang could belong to no one but Duncan Calder. I tried to speak out, lost my voice, and realized I was almost too nervous to answer him. Surely, the murderer I awaited was not this bull in a china shop! He might have killed me earlier in the night when Leander Rumford and I were helpless beneath that altar in the church interior. Mr. Rumford's lamp, with its myriad psychedelic lights, had gone out, and Duncan arrived with his flashlight. How simple to have murdered me that minute!

"Nell, answer me. Please!" The door shook under a heavy push.

I tried again to raise my voice. "What do you want? I've gone to bed."

"I must talk to you."

"Talk, then!"

"Confidential. It's confidential. A secret, old girl. Open the door like a good girl."

"Later, Duncan. In the morning."

The big fellow apparently threw himself against the door. I even heard the splintering of wood but nothing worse happened. I rushed across the room and pushed against the door on my side, praying that Keith would arrive at this all-important time. It occurred to me that I was going to feel remarkably silly if Duncan turned out to be innocent. But Keith had been explicit. I was not to let anyone in but Keith and Maddern.

Duncan gave up his strong-arm act and seemed about to retreat. I leaned against the door, weakly thankful. His voice came to me now, from further away.

"Nell, if you won't let me in, don't let anyone else in. You hear me?"

"I hear you. Don't worry. I'm locked in. Nobody can get in. Or out. Until . . . later."

"That's the lassie."

Thank heaven, he was gone! I heard his boots grating on the steps as he started down. Now, if only I had possessed that gun Keith promised me, I could have let Duncan in, waited for his first betraying move, and held him captive here until Keith and Maddern arrived. I turned tiredly, resting the back of my head against the door, and looked around at the room, the one spot in Sea Abbey that was still safe for me.

For a minute or two there was silence and a kind of warm, pink security, thanks to the lamplight. The reaction after my tense hour or two made me long for the ease and refuge of that bed against the wall between the French door and the bathroom.

The bathroom door was ajar. I hadn't noticed that before. Had Keith left the door ajar when he looked in before examining the balcony?

My heartbeat seemed to take a sudden jolt. Because Keith and I had both forgotten about the bathroom. We had forgotten it because the door was closed tightly and we had simply rushed by it to look out at the more obvious danger of that narrow ledge that was the upper level. For a few seconds I found myself so petrified with fear that I couldn't move or think. The door was moving. Only a single breath before the occupant of that dark little room came into view, I looked around frantically for a weapon. Everything sharp, even combs, my manicure kit, everything was in the bathroom. Nothing in the bedroom seemed in the least likely except the lamp on the night stand.

In the bathroom doorway Bessie Calder's thinning, fuzzy blonde hair caught the lamplight from my room. She came into the bedroom quietly, ludicrous in a nylon jumpsuit that accentuated her heavy breasts and thighs. She had one finger to her mouth, like a child hiding a secret.

"Good show, your not letting him in. He would have finished what he started last summer when he sent Granny Calder over the balcony, and all for nothing. There was no money left, not even hers."

Mentally feeling my way, but stiffly on my guard for any suspicious movement on her part, I said without the irony I felt, "And you came here to help me."

"It was the only way. I knew nobody would believe me. He needs your money so terribly, Nell. You see—" She was much closer. She did not seem to have a weapon. But one of her arms was behind her. "You see—I've used up all I had. All the money Papa left me. And Dunc always needs money . . . so you have to die. And after you, after the wedding, your brother dies. He's a nice lad, but he's got to die on account of the money, you see. Because there's no future for me at all without the money. They'd bounce me out on my ear and Dunc would divorce me so quick your head would swim. If they had no money. Because they'd send Dunc out to marry another heiress . . . do you see?"

I could hardly believe this pitiful woman was the creature who had terrified Leander and me at the altar tonight. Or was she, after all, telling the truth about it when she accused her husband? Was she warning me, even trying to protect me against this husband she adored in spite of everything?

"I see how it is," I said gently. I was afraid of her, and yet I pitied her so much I could hardly bring myself to use violence, if I must, against her. "Can't I help? Invest in the estate here? Call it a loan. A large sum. Then he wouldn't have to divorce you and marry an heiress. You wouldn't—he wouldn't have to kill me, or my brother." I warmed to the idea, to the prospect of making this madwoman see the light, if she was insane and a killer. How easily I could have been mistaken! Duncan was a much more likely killer.

She put her hand to her forehead. She was sweating, and yet it was very cold.

"What a headache! Wow! It's so damned stuffy in here! Can't we have a little air? Would you mind awfully opening the door . . . the balcony door?"

. . . I'm not that stupid, old girl! I thought. So it is you, and not Duncan! Or Emy. Or Freddie. At least, I know now where we stand . . .

"The lock is stuck. I'm afraid I forced it. I'll have

to have it fixed. I'm sorry. Could I get you a drink of water?"

She fluttered around, getting a little closer. "Honest! I swear to God I'm that hot—sweaty—you wouldn't believe it. Let's see if we can't get it open together."

I stepped backward, trying to get closer to the hall door without making it obvious that I was running away. I laughed on a high, unnatural note.

"You try the lock. I've used all the strength I can muster up."

"That's a bloody shame!" she said loudly, suddenly belligerent, her round face puffy and red. "Don't you run out on me, you rotten money-grabbing bitch!"

I knew now that there was a weapon in her concealed hand and I made a quick grab for the chair in front of the door, hoping either to throw it aside or at her before she got the weapon into action. But I heard a terrific "hiss" through the air behind me and fell flat on the floor, just in time to miss a black poker that came down hard on the chair arm, cracking the wood.

. . . Missed me again, I reminded myself, scrambling over the floor to escape the next of those powerful swings. She had apparently picked up the poker as she escaped the church interior half an hour before. I was so busy avoiding that poker and trying to protect my head that I scarcely noticed the door pressing inward, shoving the chair, the hassock, into the center of the room. Even if this was Keith, he might well be too late.

I screamed, "Keith! Keith!" and fell against the corner of the night stand, cracking my head, and was briefly stunned. Bessie raised the poker again. She had great muscular power. In an absolute panic, I reached across the night stand behind me, fumbling for something, anything my fingers could close around. They

found the base of the lamp. As Bessie brought the poker down, I hurled the lamp in her face.

The poker bounced onto the bed. Bessie hurtled
backward, shrieking wildly. I reached for her, but it
was too late. She crashed through the glass of the
French door, and by the time I crawled to her on the
little balcony, she was beyond anyone's help. She must
have died in seconds from those deadly daggers of
shattered glass.

FOURTEEN

Keith's arms pulled me back into the room, lifting me onto the tumbled bed, his stern face anxious and shocked.

"Darling! Are you all right?"

"Fine. Fine. Just a little shaky. What about Bess?"

"Duncan is with her. I'm afraid she is dead. But you! Are you sure you aren't hurt? There is blood spattered all over you." Almost at once he realized where the blood had come from and flinched a little.

I looked beyond him, seeing Duncan's great back as he huddled over his wife. The sun was already up. When had that happened? It was a watery sun, casting a hint of rusty blood-color over Sea Island and especially Duncan's bright hair. I heard an odd sound, certainly odd for Duncan, and discovered that he was weeping for the dead woman. How Bessie would have enjoyed knowing that her husband loved her, even a little!

"I'm afraid it's Bessie's blood," I told Keith in a low voice. "She confessed almost everything. She tried to make it sound as though Duncan were guilty, but she was so mixed up, she eventually threatened me herself. And by the way she swung that poker, I could see the resemblance to that ghastly business in the church last night. Mr. Maddern didn't arrive, did he?"

"No. But Duncan caught me as I was getting my revolver for you, and explained his difficulty. He had

179

tried to tell you the truth about his wife, but you wouldn't let him in. You were quite right about that, Darling. But why in heaven's name did you let Bessie come in?"

I laughed a little hysterically. "I didn't! She was there. Waiting." I explained that we had missed the bathroom in our search.

"Good God! I thought we had covered every possibility. It was a terrible secret Duncan discovered last night, although he'd begun to suspect, even accused her of wanting to be rid of you for the money. That was the night before last. He told me he had never been entirely convinced that our grandmother died of an accidental fall. Bessie had been talking too much about what we would do with her money. But, of course, there was none; and then Bessie became convinced, apparently, that the money must be gotten somewhere else, or she would lose Duncan. He had several arguments with her since you arrived. He was worried. You may imagine why, after his suspicions of Grandmother's death. The Reverend Hawkins heard that argument night before last and came up here to tell you in confidence of your danger. The climb tired him. He drank that water Bess had left for you. You know the rest."

It seemed then that the only thing we couldn't blame Bess for was Emy's bridal nerves the day I arrived; for to tell the truth, I had begun to suspect that that, too, was part of these plots at Sea Abbey. I sat up, started to speak about Duncan, then remembered his presence nearby and shut up. But he got to his feet at that minute and then we all looked around, startled, as Bob and Emy appeared in the open hall doorway, with a thousand questions. They had both dressed, obviously not guessing what caused the sudden shattering of glass a few minutes before.

While Keith explained to them what was still a puzzling nightmare to me, Constable Maddern arrived with Freddie. Almost before I could realize the nightmare was irrevocably ended. Poor Bessie's blood-drenched body was removed and we all gave our testimony to the Constable. Hours later, it still seemed to me a queer, timeless horror, but not to all of us, as it turned out.

"A happy conclusion all around," Freddie stated cheerfully as he reached for the sherry decanter. "These outrages were not committed by a Calder at all."

I did not look at Keith, but his fingers on my hand tightened with his suppressed fury. Before he could say anything, however, Bob and Emy burst out together.

"Really, Sir!"

"Oh, Father! Don't be so bloody crude!"

Freddie shrugged and waved the decanter in our direction of the lounge. Keith, Mr. Rumford and I shook our heads, but Constable Maddern politely accepted the little stem glass and put it to his lips. He then said discreetly, "I believe we've got most of the details now. The—er—lady was clearly a bit . . . off. Not quite knowing what she did, as it were."

"I'm sure it is so," I put in. I was the outsider, the catalyst for this whole tragedy. Elinor Garrison and her stupid money that had been so desperately important to Bessie Calder. Important not for the money—Bessie had never been greedy for that—but for the uses to which the money could be put, such as holding the affection of her husband.

Less than an hour after the horror of Bessie Calder's attack and her death in the tower, I had made up my mind to leave the island as soon as possible. I would remain in Abbeyvue until the investigation of the crimes at Sea Island, but I would not sleep another night on the island. I was no longer afraid, but I despised the very ease with which Bessie's death was dismissed by Freddie Calder, the master of Sea Island.

There was more discussion of how fortunate it was that things were settled now, and even Emily reminded us finally, "Don't forget, Constable, she murdered Granny."

The Constable set the sherry glass down to examine his notes. "I believe we must set that aside, Miss Emy. Proof! That's the thing. The woman more or less confessed her other crimes to Miss Garrison, but—excuse me, Ma'am," he went on to me, "we have only your word for the woman's boasts."

"Not quite, Constable," said Duncan's voice from the archway into the hall. He looked ashen, still suffering from shock. His reaction was surprising to me. I had assumed his interest in his wife was purely mercenary. "My brother has told you how I came to him and warned him about my—about Bess. But I'm guilty, too."

We all stared at him. I had a terrible premonition he was going to say that he helped his wife to plan the killings, just as Bessie had told me at first. But the truth, while not innocent, was understandable.

"I suspected—I wondered if it might have been Bess who threw down that crucifix on Nell the first night of her stay here. I saw Bess coming out of the vault that night. I should have warned Nell, as the poor devil of a vicar tried to do. We never did discover why the lights went out in the modern sector that night. There seemed to be no cause. But other than pure coincidence, it could have been Bess' work. She certainly got to Nell's sleeping capsules and emptied them into that water. And all this before the vicar went up to speak with Nell."

"Yes, but her faint, there in the hall with me the other morning," I put in.

Keith said quietly, "Duncan, I couldn't find any cause for that faint whatever. Neither could Elinor."

Duncan agreed, with a sigh. "She was afraid I might betray her, I suppose; so she pulled off that faint. I imagine she thought it would build up sympathy, make it impossible for anyone to suspect her . . . so we quarrelled. Hawkins overheard—well, you know the rest. Bess told me she's *done for* Nell, but I thought it was a bluff. Later, of course, I realized that she hoped to make Nell's death look like an overdose of her own sleeping capsules."

"And you did nothing, Sir?" Maddern asked with only a slight edge to the words.

Keith started to intercede for his brother but Duncan cut him off quickly, defensively.

"I went without sleep for two nights! I've been doing my damnedest to watch Bess. And last night, I tried to get in to protect Nell, after Bess scared her and poor Leander with the monk business in the church."

Keith added, "I had warned Elinor about opening the door to anyone. But when my brother left her, he came and warned me. We reached the tower room very nearly too late. But Elinor seems to have defended herself adequately, in spite of everything."

They went over the entire bloody story again at the Constable's insistence, but finally we were permitted to go our way, so long as we remained within reach of the courts.

I said goodbye to the island with very little reluctance. Emily and my brother would be married in Abbeyvue; so I need not miss the event which had brought me to Sea Abbey. Having kissed the two lovers who saw me off in the ancient boat with Keith, I settled stiffly on the plank seat, depressed both by the events of the past few days and by this, perhaps the final parting from Keith, except for the formalities of the wedding.

Neither of us spoke during the trip over dangerously choppy waters, until we headed in to the quay at Abbeyvue, which was noisy with Market Day. Keith was lifting me out of the rocking boat when he broke our silence by saying suddenly, "I am leaving Sea Island myself."

"I am glad." I was afraid this sounded cruel. I knew how much the discovery that he had a family must have meant to him; so I added gently, "They are living in the past. It is different with you."

He drew me closer and while I briefly hoped for something more romantic, he shook me. Hardly conducive to romance!

"Your damned money! But for that, we could be happy."

I extended my arms, touching his throat until I clasped my fingers at the nape of his neck. People were watching us, but to my way of thinking, this only sealed what I was contriving. I grazed my lips against his, and proceeded from there to pressures that would make him remember our parting kiss so long that he would be unable to dredge up any more tiresome scruples against rich women.

I was aided, no end, by the interested citizens of Abbeyvue.

About the Author

With over 5½ million books sold, Virginia Coffman is surely one of the most popular Gothic authors today. The author of numerous books published in both paperback and hardcover in the United States and in Europe, Virginia Coffman has also been published in magazines and has had one of her short stories adapted for the Paris stage. Film rights have been purchased for two of her Gothic novels.

Miss Coffman was born in San Francisco and spent most of her adult life in Hollywood, first as a secretary during the Howard Hughes years at RKO and later as a script editor. She now lives in Reno, Nevada, and pursues her hobbies of reading and making yearly trips to Europe. Virginia Coffman is a continuing author for NAL. Among her titles have been *Black Heather, Castle at Witches' Coven,* and *The House on the Moat.*

Other SIGNET Gothics You'll Enjoy
